The woods of white

Written by D. B. Sherratt

Author

Copyright © 2024 by D. B. Sherratt.

All rights reserved.

No part of this publication may be reproduced, distributed, or transmitted in any form or by any means, including photocopying, recording, or other electronic or mechanical methods, without the prior written permission of the publisher. For permission requests, contact D. B. Sherratt.

The story, all names, characters, and incidents portrayed in this production are fictitious. No identification with actual persons (living or deceased), places, buildings, and products are intended or should be inferred.

Book Cover Design by Alysha Davison, Tom Pepper and Bryan Dowley.

Copyedit and proofread by Hazel Walshaw and Michelle Lomas.

CONTENT WARNINGS:

Please refer to the last page to see warning details. This is to avoid potential spoilers for readers.

ACKNOWLEDGEMENTS

For my father, who always believed I could make it as an author and counted down to see the day I publish my work. Thank you for always believing in me.

For my mother, who taught me empathy and brought me up to be the understanding woman I have become. Thank you for being my teacher.

For my older sister, who provided visual examples of what would get me into trouble. Thank you for making me wise.

For my younger sister, who would enjoy reading books I wrote at a young age. Thank you for being my first fan.

For my partner, who kept pushing me to continue, even when times did get hard. Thank you for being my encouragement.

For my local writing club, who had me pinned up in the corner until I wrote them an acknowledgement. Thank you for also being my support group.

The woods of white

Five stages of grief

Water trickled down the transparent glass. Each droplet unique, just like the snowflake, and when the mind is not distracted, all you can hear and see is the rain in all its peaceful and calming nature. I followed one drop down as it connected to another and configured a pattern of a dancing ballerina. I gazed at the shape in grief, as even nature could prove that during its darkest and most dangerous time, it can present just a slight shimmer of happiness in its own way.

I am usually a positive minded person, but like most people, I need time to myself to cry. I have a very good reason for needing this time to cry to myself. The weight of negativity had led me to pessimistic thoughts. Death is a funny thing. Through these terrible thoughts, I have learned to find that death is a lot like sleeping. It is a moment of rest and peace, when all the pain and torment has finally left. However, for those who still remain awake... Well, they then carry on the pain and torment. Death dwells where suffering is present, but also creates suffering for those around the presence of death.

You truly don't know the mental impact until someone very close to you has passed away. You can imagine it, yes. You can imagine days of crying, buying boxes of tissues and finding peace by being with family or friends... But this is not even close. It doesn't even touch the foundation of how it affects a person. The reality is that you feel as though your heart is about to give up on you. Your lungs feel the heaviest that they have ever done before, and your throat feels swollen, making your cries silent as your vocals become enclosed. This isn't even for an hour, maybe two… This is through the nights. Your eyes become heavy, bags begin appearing, as you no longer have a peaceful night's sleep. This is the reality.

    The crying stopped for a moment, to allow the headache to disperse temporarily. I lay back in my chair, massaging the temples of my head, trying to provide some self-control. Just two hours earlier, before writing these words with pen and paper, I was removing the razor head from its arm in an attempt to slice it against the fair skin on my wrist. At the point when I was about to harm myself, I had a sudden conscious experience, which now makes me wonder if a person committing suicide would think to themselves before taking their own life. In that moment I thought, what will this accomplish? I know better than this to overcome my anger at the loss I have suffered.

    This is when I took my blank notepad and a black biro to start writing my feelings. This keeps my mind focused on paper rather than hurting myself. I can relive the memories in these words; the good times and the worst times. And, after completing this journal, I can bring closure to my hurt and pain. I can start to relive my life. It will never be the same, but I can at least try.

Learning from mistakes

As the orange sun set in the clear sky, its light penetrated the window, reflecting from my mirror into my eyes. Closing the blinds, I cut out the natural light, replacing it with something artificial. The bright LED lights that surrounded my mirror brought out any imperfections on my skin, making it easier to hide the scars.

Footsteps strutted up the stairs in a slow, tormenting pattern. My body tensed and I lowered my eyeshadow palette to the desk, looking at my closed door through the reflection of my mirror.

Matthew marched into the room, providing a dominant approach. This was not an unusual sight, as he took this presentation when wanting to tower above me, so I would follow his rules and regulations. After all, he was 'the man of the house'.

After ten years together, I have only recently identified the red flags of my relationship. A relationship is always amazing at the beginning. The butterflies in your stomach, the feeling of something new and exciting. Having the opportunity to learn about each other and enjoy their company. Then the first fight breaks out. You choose to be the mature person and accept, forgive, and move on with life. How many times do they have to make the mistake for us to notice the red flag? For some, they may have picked up on it early through experience. For others, they may absorb more pain before realising the harsh truth of their so called 'love'.

Some partners can be sneaky with their red flags. They may hide their torture behind mental impact, rather than physical. This can be presented in ways such as guilt-tripping. Unfortunately, this is something that I have become all too comfortable with. All these years I felt as though my partner was looking out for me, when in reality, he used guilt-tripping as a way of keeping me away from the world.

I started to recognise the corrupt ways of my relationship when I became closer with an old friend, Bernadette. Matthew grew overprotective, not allowing me to leave the house unless he was near. I had tried to talk to Matthew and help him to understand my feelings, but he would shut the conversation down. Immaturely, Matthew would leave the house and upon returning, would refuse to talk to me for not hours, but days. This was until we could both forget the conversation and move on.

Bernadette had tried to bring up the strength in me to leave my partner, but how could I? We had been together for ten years, got engaged, bought a house and we were preparing for a wedding that seemed to be further and further away, every time we brought it up. To give up so far down the line after so much sacrifice and accomplishments, just for my own happiness, seemed almost stupid. The more I thought about the situation, the more I wondered if I really would be happier if I left my partner. It would mean I'd have to start my life over. I would have to go back to my parents. I would have to look at renting somewhere and, with only one income, I wouldn't be able to afford more than a one-bedroom terraced property. Would it even be worth it? Would I lie in depression as I started a life on my own? I have been in a relationship since my late teens. It's all I have ever known as I matured into an adult.

Matthew stood behind me, staring at me through the reflection of the glass. I met with his eyes, reciprocating the same dominant approach. I refused to divert my eyes to anywhere but him. I couldn't allow Matthew to see any weakness in me. This approach angered him, as he continued to march towards me, until he was towering above me at the makeup desk.

"I've thought about what you said and considering Bernadette is only holding a small, *all girl's* birthday party, I am happy for you to go."

I looked at him through the reflection with relief that he was allowing me to visit Bernadette on her birthday. Picking up the palette, I prepared to continue getting myself ready.

"I have a few conditions, though," he continued. "I will drop you off and I will pick you up at 11pm."

"11pm?" I questioned his harsh conditions.

Matthew sat down on the bed beside me, holding one hand over my back, stroking softly.

"April, you know how I feel about you getting into a taxi, alone. At least if I pick you up, I know you'll be safe. I don't want to be leaving any later than 11pm, though. I need to be up for work in the morning. That should give you plenty of time!"

Feeling partially annoyed, I was happy enough that I was able to attend a party alone, without Matthew being there. Nodding my head, Matthew leaned across, smiling, and kissed me on the forehead before leaving the room.

I always knew that Matthew never truly liked Bernadette. He never admitted to it, but I imagined it was down to Bernadette's chosen lifestyle. She was abused by her father as a child and lost all respect for men as she grew up. Bernadette never truly accepted Matthew as my partner. Many times, she would say, "Who needs a man? Women can do everything they can and more if they just put their minds to it. Men are 100% replaceable now, thanks to the likes of sex stores". It would often make me laugh, but she was right in everything she said, except for one thing… I never would have experienced the true meaning of intimacy without love. I am a firm believer that everything happens for a reason. Whether it is good or bad, it leads us to where we need to be.

Matthew dropped me off around the corner from Bernadette's home. He came to a stop, putting the gear into neutral and faced me, as I picked up the bottle of gin from the footwell.

"Remember, 11pm," he imprinted onto my brain.

I rolled me eyes and nodded, kissing him on the lips before exiting the car. I brushed down my dress and looked at the house, which had colourful lights glowing through the windows. Her home always reminded me of a little fairy house. There was no drive, just a narrow pathway overhung by ivy that twisted around a metal garden arch. The pathway led towards a heavy oak front door. Although her home was small, Bernie made the most of the space she had. It appeared the party had already started. Bernadette always liked to be loud in her appearance. She painted that across her house as there were balloons tied to the pillars of her front gate and a bright pink banner stuck across her oak door reading "30th Birthday Girl". Typical Bernie!

I waited until Matthew had driven past, before knocking. I didn't want Bernadette to see that he had dropped me off. I was worried enough about telling her I only had until 11pm. Even Cinderella had longer at the ball. I waved Matthew off until the brake lights had stopped glowing at the end of the road.

"April!" Bernadette hollered with open arms. I shared the same welcome, feeling happier to be there.

"I thought this was only a small gathering, Bernie?" I asked.

Her chuckle was outrageous. It was one that could be recognised from miles away. Bernadette swayed her head back to the crammed house and back to me with one pointy eyebrow raised. Pointing down at her pinned 30th birthday badge, I realised that I was in no position to question who and how she wanted to celebrate such a big milestone.

Ironically, turning thirty didn't make her anymore responsible, as she started pouring vodka in a cup, in an attempt to catch me up with the others.

Watching the time closely, I became paranoid, counting down the minutes I had left. More and more people came flooding in through the door. A lot of the faces I barely recognised from our younger years. As time went on, disappointment radiated over my face, wishing time would just stop for one moment.

"You're not leaving early!"

Bernadette had one arm folded over her chest and a drink in the other hand. She raised her eyebrows and looked down at me with her command.

"I can't stay late, Bernie. He's coming for me at 11pm."

"Fuck him! Stay in my spare room tonight. If he knocks on, then I just won't open the door."

I laughed at her response. That's all I could do. I wanted to stay so bad, but I also didn't want to upset my boyfriend.

Hands began clapping for attention in the living room. "C'mon! Let's play a drinking game, everyone. Let's liven this sad bunch up a bit."

I didn't recognise his face when I made my way into the living room. I was met by the jade green eyes of a tall, dark-haired man. He caught me looking and returned the look with half of a smirk covering his face. If moments like this had happened whilst I was sober, my face would have turned as bright red as my hair. But I'd had a few drinks, so my confidence was high at the time. (Probably something I'd regret in the morning).

People began gathering around in the living room, waiting for further instruction. I watched as he lifted a bottle of whisky. He started shaking it in his right arm and with a cheeky smile he said the words, "Never have I ever..." He looked around the room as everyone began chuckling. As he observed the room, his eyes met mine yet again. He opened his mouth very slightly, showing his perfect white teeth.

"I think we could all learn a little bit about each other tonight," he added.

People began circling as this unknown, mysterious, yet very intriguing man began filling up cups with any spirit he could find lying around the house.

"Never have I ever... drunk dialled my ex," he began. He glanced around the room as he watched more people than not take a drink from their cup. I considered this starting statement to be pretty innocent, compared to my usual 'Never have I ever' experiences. I listened and the further along the circle we went, the dirtier the statements became. It came to my turn, and I forgot to think of something before it got around to me.

"Come on redhead, I bet you can think of something *naughty*," he piped up.

No matter how much drink I'd had, that comment still made me feel warm to my face...

No, God no, don't start turning red now.

"Never have I ever... had sex in an outdoor public place." I watched as he took a large drink from his cup, along with many others who were invisible to me at that point, except for him.

I became distracted as I saw the front screen of my phone brighten to the side of my leg.

Matthew: I'm outside.

No kisses and he hasn't even got out of the car to knock on at the house. I knew immediately that he was annoyed with me for being out on Bernadette's birthday. I picked up my phone quickly to start texting back.

Me: I'll be out soon; I'm just playing a game. Won't be long. Love you xx

Matthew: I have already lost sleep waiting up for you to finish off at this party. The least you could do is grab your stuff and come out now.

Looking down at my phone in anger, I clenched my phone harder in my hand. As I began standing, Bernadette interrupted, "You're not leaving, are you? It isn't even midnight!"

I gave her a certain look back, which is the look we both know as 'you already know the answer'. I continued to stand and apologised to everyone for my quick disappearance. "I'm so sorry, Bernadette, but you know he's outside waiting for me."

"Well tell him to come in for a bit then. We haven't even made it around the full circle of this game yet."

"He wants to head off, Bernie. It's OK."

"No, it's not!" she bellowed.

Bernadette stood up as quickly as her legs would let her on numerous shots of spirit. She headed for her front door as I tried to pull her back. The last thing I wanted was drama. I could never stand arguments or disagreements.

Bernadette opened her front door and made her voice loud enough for the street to hear, "Oi! Prick! It's my birthday, so you can either stop being a sulky bitch and come in to be social, or you can fuck off back home!"

Dear God, no... She doesn't understand what she's done to me.

I watched as Matthew started up his car and sped off down the street as loud as he possibly could. My heart sank as I dreaded to think of how much trouble I would be in when I returned home.

"Looks like you're stopping mine tonight, April."

I couldn't even pull a smile for her. I hated her for this. I hated her for intervening with my relationship. I spun around to storm back into the house, when I saw him standing in the doorway with his shoulder leaned against the door frame.

"Seems like a prick to me, too," he agreed. "Let's get some more drinks, hey?"

My heart started beating faster and my hands began shaking with anxiety. Did Matthew see him standing there and think the worst of the situation? Or was he just annoyed with Bernie? I tried to block the worst thoughts from my head. I've managed to get my way for once and I am still here having a laugh with my best friend. What could go wrong?

The night continued and thankfully, I did start enjoying myself again without thinking of home. The only thing I couldn't understand was if it was the drink making me happier, or him. I wandered back to the kitchen for another refill. Bernie was chomping down on some nuggets that she put in the oven a little earlier.

"Who is he?" I asked Bernadette.

"Who? The guy you keep gawping at?"

I shot my head straight up to look at her. She shook the plastic cup around in one hand with her pinky sticking out at the bottom. She couldn't help smiling, as much as she tried staying serious.

"Don't think I haven't noticed!" she exclaimed.

"Alright… Well, what's his name?"

"Casey. He used to work at the phone shop with me. He's a lovely guy… Definitely knows his way around the bedroom," she winked at me.

"Oh, have you… With Casey?"

Bernadette blurted out a laughter and wiped her mouth from the outrageous expression of alcohol dripping from her mouth.

"No, I'm only joking. Although I have heard it from one of the girls I used to work with."

I tried processing this information, although I'm still not sure why. I have never once thought about having a life with anyone except Matthew. Despite that, with the constant arguments recently and because of the way Casey had been so intriguing to me, I was afraid that I was on the look for a "greener side" subconsciously.

"You can't tell me you've never had sex outside, Red," he said with a deep and yet drunk voice.

My eyes widened as I didn't realise he was behind me listening. Or was he listening? Has he only just come into the kitchen? At this point it was 2am and most people had left to return to their homes, except for me…

"You can't sneak up on a girl like that!" I exclaimed.

Bernie just nodded her head with laughter like a villainous bobble head.

"Maybe so, but you still haven't answered me."

"Don't need to. It was a game."

He stood in silence for a moment at my pushback and he looked at Bernie for support.

"Do you want another drink, Casey? I've got plenty left in here."

Thank God, Bernadette changed the topic.

"Well, that's why I initially come in here, but then I spotted two lovely ladies chatting away."

Lovely ladies – Why did that make me feel like a giddy child?

Before I could even realise, the whole night had disappeared in front of us, while me and a few others drunkenly opened up to each other about our lives. I felt even more guilty as I realised how much I was pulling Matthew down in front of some people that I barely knew in that room. Matthew wasn't always this horrible person that I portray to you all now. There have been so many happy memories that I had built with him, but the little red flags began growing and I couldn't hold back my anger anymore. It started off as an explanation to everyone to provide reasoning for my early departure, but I continued on regarding the other issues in my life. Along with the guilt, I also felt a moment of release and warmth. Sharing in other people's experiences felt like being in a therapy session.

But Casey, he didn't say much. The odd nod of the head and little comments made here and there, but I still knew nothing about him, and I felt eager to know more. This just played on my conscience more and more, as I tried to push possible ideas and future opportunities aside.

That was not me!

Don't let the anchor be your burden

I probably had about two or three hours sleep that night and it was spent on the sofa, cuddling up to Bernadette. The few that were left after a night of gaming and gossiping were still there. Even though it wasn't my house, I felt the need to assist Bernadette as the host.

We put together some breakfast baps and coffee for everyone to help with their hangover.

As much as I tried to stay in the moment, my mind kept taking me to thoughts about the near future. How I am getting home and what will happen when I do get home? My hands started shaking nervously. This isn't healthy, I shouldn't feel this way. People were able to have a laugh and enjoy themselves, even with a hangover, so why is it that I feel so scared?

I know why. Stop being stupid, April.

I checked my phone for messages, but there was nothing. Not a check in, no text to ask if I need picking up or even an apology. I blew out a loud and well-needed sigh, rolling my eyes into the cushions of the sofa.

"You know what my dad once told me, red?"

I already knew who asked the question, even though my face was still indented within the sofa's Febreeze scent.

"Don't think I was there when you were growing up with your dad, so not entirely sure. Go on…"

Did that sound like a rude response? It wasn't meant to be.

Again, with his half smirk… It made him all the more mysterious, as though he were hiding something. I couldn't see the full picture, not yet.

"Life is like an anchor."

I cocked my head to one side with my upper lip slightly raised. For the life of me, I couldn't understand where he was going with this, but I was somewhat intrigued.

"An anchor's purpose is to steady the ship in place. It can't move again unless the chain for the anchor is lifted. Red, you'll never be able to move to your wanted destination if that anchor stays down. Do you understand?"

I knew exactly what he meant, and that's what wounded me the most. I already knew what was weighing me down in the dark depths. I already knew why I was stuck in this mental state of despair, but I couldn't lift that anchor. Ten years it's been holding me down in the unforeseen and I wasn't sure if I had the strength in me to be able to budge it. Instead of this response, I just nodded my head, looking down. I held a cup of freshly made hot coffee between both hands, whilst tapping my engagement ring against the ceramic.

About an hour or two passed before Bernadette drove me back home.

"I only care about you, April," she reassured me whilst the music echoed from the car's speakers.

"I know and thank you, but…"

"But what?"

"I have to make the choice from here. I'll take the path that I need to."

Bernadette kept her eyes focused on the road, but leaned into the passenger side to briefly rest her head on my shoulder.

"I know you will, Red," she whispered.

I snorted at her comment, but it was nothing to take notice of. Not when I had more pressing matters playing on my mind.

We pulled up along my street, but something wasn't right. Where was Matthew's car?

Stop overthinking April! You always do this to yourself. He's probably nipped out to the shop to get milk, or bread. Yes, that's got to be it… Right?

"Do you want me to come in with you and help calm things?" Bernadette asked with pure sincerity.

"Thank you, but I think it's better that I try to resolve it with him on my own."

"Don't let the anchor be your burden, Red. I love you!"

"I love you, too," I sincerely repeated back as I got out of her vehicle and closed the car door.

I reached into my handbag to get the keys from the front pocket. It wasn't until I tried unlocking the front door that I realised how much I had started uncontrollably shaking. *How hard is it to unlock a bloody door? Just. Go. In!*

The door swung open and at that precise moment, I forgot how to walk. It was as though my involuntary shaking had coursed its way through my body, making me unknowingly paralysed. I tried to take a step forward, but rather than a step, my mind and body collapsed.

Four full bin bags sat against the wall of the hallway. Each bag contained my clothes and other belongings. There was no sign of Matthew anywhere, but even if he was in the house, I couldn't gain the strength to stand and look around. Even if he was standing in front of me in that moment, I wouldn't be able to see him as my eyes became a flooded blur.

I can't remember how long I was lying on the hallway floor, but I knew it was long enough for pins and needles to start setting into my feet and legs. My sleeve became soaked through as my head lay on it whilst I curled up on my side, just trying to understand what was going on.

What did I do to deserve this? I replayed the night over and over in my head and sat myself down on trial to question every action I made last night and gave myself an answer.

Q: Why did I look back and acknowledge Casey?

A: But Matthew wasn't there and doesn't know about my interactions with Casey and even if he was, what I did wasn't immoral. I did nothing wrong.

Q: Why did I tell everyone about my relationship issues?

A: Again, Matthew wasn't there at that time, but even if he was, I would tell him that the only reason I am expressing my feelings to these people is because he won't let me express the issues to him.

Q: What if Matthew saw Casey in the doorway and assumed the worst?

A: Then Matthew should have simply asked me so I could prove to him that nothing had or would happen.

That's it. I had answered my own questions, and each answer just proved his immaturity to want to resolve and strengthen this relationship. It was always his way or no way, and this was the final straw. If he wanted me out, then I would be more than happy to comply with that. This was it. This was the moment I had been waiting for, but I had been too weak to do it myself.

I steadied myself up against the wall and marched into the kitchen to grab my car key. That's when my eyes caught sight of the note. An A4 paper ripped from a pad and words scribbled down in anger. The shaking started up again, but this time it wasn't nerves, it was rage.

All of your belongings are packed. Take them anywhere but here. I don't want to wake up next to your lying face again.

Don't think I didn't see him standing inside the door. What happened to a small girly gathering? What other lies have you been telling me all these years? I saw the way he looked at you...

The amount I have sacrificed for us, and this is how you repay me?

I'm stopping at my parents until 8pm and I want you out with all your stuff before then.

I screwed the paper up in my hand and bellowed out a scream before hitting my fist against the worktop. My outrage got the better of me this time, and tears began flooding again.

Is this what he's been telling people? I'm the problem? How many of our friends has he already sided up against me since last night? How much exaggeration has he portrayed on what was actually seen? It's too much to think about and too much that can't be answered without overthinking and adding to the pain. All I did know was that I wished he was here, so I could finally have *my* say.

I can! I can have my say. He is at his parents, just the next town over.

With the scrunched-up piece of paper in one hand, my car key in the other and a mind full of agony, I took my belongings to my Golf Mk 1. I started the engine, making my way to Matthew's parents' house.

As I started approaching the street, I hit a wall. This is the same mental wall a runner would face during a marathon. The body becomes unruly. Their legs turn to jelly, yet they feel as though they weigh more than their entire body weight. Their physical body comes to a stop. I stopped. What was I doing?

Get out of this mind block, April. You know exactly why you are here. You know how many times you have tried to be reasonable. The patience held back to tolerate the anger from someone who acted as though all they did was love you.

Now it was my turn to raise my voice and with that loud beckoning voice, I managed to force myself through that brick wall and onto a greener side. Just. Don't. Hesitate.

I turned off my ignition and slammed my car door shut. With the amount of rust hanging on that Golf, I'm surprised my door didn't fall off its hinges.

As I stormed towards the front door, Matthew's mother stood there. I never properly gained a healthy relationship with her, either. Matthew was an only child, and I always felt that his mum thought I was taking him from her. I was never invited around for tea, even after the engagement. She always criticised me and my family, but not to my face. She didn't have the bravery to say it to my face, but to other people behind my back was absolutely fine. Just as I did with Matthew, I brushed her comments under the rug, never to look back on it again. Now, though, the dirt was piling up, and it was slowly spilling out from the edges of the rug with nowhere else to go. It was time that I picked up the dirt and dumped it in the bin.

"Matthew has already made his point that he doesn't want you around." His mother's destructive voice echoed down the drive towards me.

"Not without a chance to have my say!" I bellowed with my hands still enclosed. My fingernails digging into the palms of my hands and my eyebrows narrowed.

I could tell at this point that Matthew's mum was in shock at my reaction, but she stood in the centre of the door making sure I couldn't pass her. Matthew's dad then appeared behind.

Rob always treated me better. I often looked at that man like he was in a similar position to me in the relationship – just nod along with your partner and do whatever they ask. I never heard that man say much. He had always been quiet, but I could tell he held a lot of his emotions deep inside. How he had never managed to blow a gasket in all of those years, I will never truly understand.

"Julia, let the girl in. At least let her talk!" His supportive, dominating demand brought Matthew's mother back inside the doorway.

I stopped my glare, and my emotions started scrambling with my mind again, as I found comfort in the fact that Matthew's dad was there too.

I brushed past Julia and looked up at Rob with a smile and tears filling my eyes. I felt his comforting hand rub my back as he showed me into the living room.

Matthew was sitting, staring at the TV. His possessive eyes met mine and he threw his arms down on the sofa.

"Thanks for the support, dad!"

"No, you listen here. You can sit there and listen to this girl."

I made my way to the armchair in the corner, so that I was facing Matthew on the sofa. I then regretted my chosen battleground. I felt vulnerable with all eyes facing me. I was on trial about to be questioned, and I was about to have my next step chosen for me.

There's that wall again. Every bit of anger and reason I had disappeared from my mind. I tried so hard to think through all the emotions to understand again why I was there and what I wanted to say. My mind could not physically comprehend everything that had happened in just the last 18 hours. Then the first comment was made.

"Since this room is more silent than a library on a quiet day, I suppose I best say that I think your behaviour, April, is completely out of the ordinary. You have both worked so hard over all these years and you pack it all in for some man." Julia stampeded through the battlefield with very little evidence, apart from the words that came from her own unruly son.

That was the comment I needed. I just needed something to rile me up again so that all my thoughts and opinions could come trembling into one. Is that what Matthew had told his parents? I cheated? The one-sided accusation. The one comment that could make the entire world turn against me without having a second hearing. This was why I was here. This was why I needed to finally have my say before leaving for good.

I looked up at Matthew, who clearly knew he was in the wrong and somehow, deep down, I think he knew that he was lying to himself. He knew that I would never cheat, as his eyes skittered around the room to look at anything but me.

My whole body tensed as I tried to sustain the trembling anger. The temperature rose in my body, like the sun gleaming through a broken piece of glass onto a defenceless insect below. I could not control my physical pain, and I wasn't able to control the words that fell from my mouth. I had always been shy, so when confronted, I hesitated. I take a moment to think carefully about how each word could impact how people perceive me. That filter had been chucked aside, along with the dirt from under the rug.

"Is that what Matthew has told you?"

I narrowed my eyes in his direction as he kept his head down and out of involvement. He knew what was best for him at that moment.

"If that man sitting in the corner had just talked to me for even a second, I would have explained to him that it was a small *all girls* gathering. In fact, I have the conversation on my phone from Bernie if you really want the proof!"

I chucked my phone in front of my audience, onto their coffee table.

"I have never met that man before in my life. I didn't even know who he was until last night. He's an old work friend of Bernadette's and considering it's her 30th, I think she's entitled to invite whoever she wants to celebrate that moment with her."

My breathing became shortened, and my mind went light. I tried to gather enough oxygen from the room to be able to continue with my concluding statement.

"This is your issue, Matthew, and it always has been. I have just been patient enough to brush that dirt under the carpet for far too long. It is always your way or no way. I am never allowed to be anywhere unless you are there to spy on me. I feel trapped in a relationship from the outside world… But Matthew…"

He slowly lifted his head until his eyes met with mine.

"Thank you for this final push to help me make the right decision."

I pulled the engagement ring from my finger and chucked it in his direction. The room fell completely silent except for the ring that bounced onto the wooden table. I took this as my time to leave, as their heads bowed in humiliation.

Looking back, I wondered if Matthew's dad heard what I had to say and that triggered a moment of realisation for him. We were both trapped in a relationship whereby we could never do anything right for our partner and we had to do as we were told. If we didn't do as we were told, the guilt trip came in. Matthew and his mum were terrible for it, but I hoped and prayed that wherever they both went with their lives that they had listened to me and made the necessary changes. I wasn't done quite yet, though. I still had one more thing to say before I left that house for the very last time.

"Rob?"

I received a last heart-warming look from Matthew's dad. He intently listened, just as he always had.

"Don't let the anchor be your burden too," I warned him.

New beginnings

I opened my eyes, looking up at the artex ceiling, which had a soft glow of warmth against the brilliant white paint. I stretched my whole body and felt the metal bar at the end of my single bed. *That's cold!* I brought my legs back up to my chest for warmth.

Rolling over to my side, the awful pink and off-white colours in the room, reminded me I was in my old childhood room. I rolled my eyes at my hideous choice of colours for a child. This was just one of the setbacks I now had to deal with, but it did help me understand myself again. This was my golden opportunity to find the real me, not the woman I was made to become. It became my time to focus on myself and only myself; to become the independent person my parents wanted me to be all along.

I changed out of my pyjamas and placed them in the washing basket next to my old drawer. My eyes rested on an old moneybox that my parents had bought me years ago. I laughed as I felt the weight of what must have been over 300 copper coins still in there.

Everyone grows up in a different household. The way we are treated and taught as a child will mirror the person we develop into as an adult. My parents were always strict, but fair. As a child, I hated this, but I learned to appreciate it more as I matured. I was always taught by my parents that if I wanted something, then I need to earn it and work for it myself. With that, I would also learn to appreciate what I had more, if I paid for it myself. If I broke it, that's on me. This was also the same response I got when I first came home and told my parents that I had left Matthew. I was welcomed back, but it wasn't a happy welcome. I put into that relationship and gave up my own independence. Now that it was broken, it was up to me to make that right. In that sense, my parents were subtly trying to tell me that I shouldn't be back at their home. I should find my own place to be that independent woman again and find my own way through life, not to hold back as a burden on my parents.

I had been on several websites over the past few days, trying to find anything in my local area to rent. There had been a few lovely spots, but before I could get a viewing in, they were off the market again. I flicked through pages on my phone whilst sat at the dining table for breakfast. My thumb stopped on one property. It was only one bedroom, but it was charming. A one-bedroom terraced cottage on a quiet road. I checked everything I could online – Only posted in the last 24 hours, only a 20-minute drive away from here. There wasn't a front garden, but there was resident permit parking available in front of the property. However, the biggest thing for me was that it was actually within my planned budget!

I picked up my phone straight away to call for a booking and, to my delight, I was advised that I could visit that same day.

Things are starting to look up. Hang on in there, April.

***

Some few weeks and signed paperwork later, I managed to call that little terraced cottage my home. My parents were ecstatic for me, but I knew my dad was just happy that I had my own place and became the independent daughter that he always wanted me to be. For the first time since I left Matthew, I was also happier in myself and the feeling of having my own furniture and my own safe space made me feel like I had made an achievement.

The only time I wasn't at my happiest was at night. That was when the loneliness really crept in through the creaking oak doors. I no longer had the comfort of knowing my parents were just across the upstairs landing. Unlocking my phone, my eyes instantly squinted, trying to block out the brightness in the dark empty room.

1:16am! When will I ever be able to fall asleep?

I rolled onto my back, staring straight up at the ceiling with a deep, irritated sigh. Knowing that I needed to be up at 6am for work provoked me even more. My eyes slowly investigated the room. Even the darkest night sky can still shed just a bit of light to evoke shadows in the room with me. The longer I stared into the shadow of my hung dressing gown against the wall, the more the shadow became an acquaintance in the room with me. It didn't move, didn't speak, but the shadow was enough for me to start closing my eyes to drift off into a deep sleep.

The mornings provided a new perception of the world. The birds had woken with me, and their calling and singing provided comfort.

I really need a pet.

I was leaving through the door for work when I completed my final checks:

Lanyard, Notebook, Laptop, Purse, Pads (can never be too careful) … Phone! Where's my phone?

I rushed back upstairs to pull my phone off charge when I saw a missed text.

Bernie: Hope you're getting on OK sweet? I was wondering if you wanted to go on a walk and have a coffee around Biddulph Moor this Saturday?

Me: Of course! We're long overdue for a catch up!

***

Over the past few weeks at work, my mind had been anywhere but focused on teaching. I had deadlines to meet, and children to help grow. Little did my pupils know that these years would be the easiest years of their life. As much as my lack of motivation and broken mind frustrated me, it was a time for me to reminisce on my own life and set goals for the near future. I began writing in my notepad about everything I knew that went wrong with Matthew. I tried to understand what I could have done better. I knew that if I was to end up in a relationship again, I must speak up more and I needed to note the red flags as quickly as they appear. To do this, I set myself little reminders. Writing became my new best friend. I became controlled by my own sticky notes that hung around the house. It was my way of being able to become the best version of myself.

A yellow sticky note with black writing hung from my fridge door. It was held in place by an old metallic Volkswagen Golf magnet, to stop it from unsticking and falling to the floor. This was the only reminder I had with a meaningful acronym which I created one night when I struggled to sleep.

If you are to take anything away from this journal, please remember to keep climbing the steep ASCENT to a healthy relationship:

1. Affection
2. Sex
3. Communication
4. Empathy
5. Notice
6. Trust

Without these 6 key strengths, a relationship will struggle and, rather than climbing the peak further, the progression will come to a halt. From there, the individual will choose to descend to the bottom and move away from the goal.

Affection – Both partners in a relationship must be able to feel a sense of devotion towards each other. To be able to sit in complete silence and look at each other, knowing each feature and the feel of contentment towards each other. If you are in a relationship, what is the colour of your partner's eyes? Can you tell me without looking?

Sex – This may seem like an obvious factor, but it is more important than you may think. If it was up to me, this would be priority one, but then I couldn't make the acronym *ASCENT*. Sex shows the physical attraction you have for your partner. This is a way in which you are able to bond with your partner on a much deeper level and to understand each other's pleasures. It further increases the emotional intimacy between two people. This doesn't have to be boring and can be changed up or interpreted in your own way and in a way which is enjoyed by your partner.

Communication – This is a factor which is most commonly dismissed. How do you deal with disputes? Do you ignore your partner? Do you hold in your thoughts over and over before exploding all at once? This only creates tension and misunderstanding between two people. No matter how small you may think some details may be, ALWAYS open up to your partner about your feelings. If you don't talk about the issues, your partner will never know how it affects you.

Empathy – This isn't just a factor for women, although it is more common for women to present feelings of empathy. This should be used no matter what the situation is. It gives us a deeper understanding about the other person and gives us the opportunity to be able to respond to their needs as best as we can.

Notice – Make sure you acknowledge your partner. Praise them when they are proud of something they have done. Sympathise with them at times of distress. Remember the small details about your partner and their likes. You will see just how much they appreciate you when you bring it up in conversation. From time to time, provide small, meaningful gifts without occasion or purpose. This spontaneity will no doubt enhance joy in your partner.

Trust – Some may be broken from past trauma and trust can, therefore, be a difficult factor. This is why you must communicate any difficulties with your partner, so that they can likewise reassure you and prove themselves to be trustworthy.

Through reading the following pages, you will learn from my story and how I managed to use these key factors to remain strong, even in the most difficult of times.

A walk to remember

The sky was deceitful. The sun glared down beneath the autumn brown leaves, but the bite of frost took its toll.

I kneeled in the dirt, the soil soaking up into my denim jeans. In front was one of my favourite trees in the wood, the Alder tree. It had stood for many years and has fought through appalling weather in quiet obedience to the same basic forces that have always governed its existence. Its leaves ever-knowingly dropped in number. Many of its branches stood naked to the tolerance of the bitter cold.

I held the camera in front of my eyes to capture nature's change. As the frost pierced through the roots of the surrounding trees, their leaves grew weak and brittle. Even the strongest of the living need time to break, but it is never forever. As I focused the camera, I registered heavy movement coming closer. I lowered the camera to see Bernadette waiting patiently for us to move on.

"Come on!" she exclaimed. "You act like you've never walked around Biddulph Grange Country Park before."

Bernadette was always dressed to impress, but the most envious part was that she put in little to no effort to look the way she does. Her bright blonde hair hung just below her shoulders. It was always perfectly straight, unlike my red, frizzy mess. She wore pink, fluffy earmuffs to stay warm with her pale pink puffer coat covering her arms. She leaned to one side so all her weight was on her right leg. Her arms remained crossed as she raised an eyebrow impatiently at me.

"Every single day is different here," I explained. "My dad

taught me that when I was young. The weather always changes and so does nature with it…"

"Alright little Miss Nature girl," she ridiculed.

I snorted, rolling my eyes before looking back up at the Alder tree. The sun pierced through the unconcealed branches to reveal its fragility. She had seen so much through her years. The time spent on Earth had made her warm and forgiving. Her remaining years are spent making us come to focus on what she can do here and now and the help she serves to all around. As death approaches every day, this is the only completely real thing in the world.

Click

I looked down at my camera to see the moment caught in a memory. I kneeled to pick up my rucksack before looking to see Bernadette stood with the same impatient expression and a smirk on her face as she mocked me.

"In fact, stay there for just a moment," she commanded.

I stood back with a muddled look on my face. She reached into her pocket for her phone, the camera facing me.

"Oh God, no!" I hid behind my hands and shielded my face from the camera.

"Shut up, April! Your hair and outfit look amazing against the autumn trees. It's as if you dressed yourself this morning to be a model in the woods. Now stay still and at least smile."

I moved my hands from my face and panicked trying to think of my posture. I lifted my knee up so my right foot was facing in on the point of my toes and my hands moved to my mustard yellow beanie hat in an attempt to pull it down over my face.

"Adorable!" Bernie added.

Adorable? I don't want adorable... I want someone to say I'm beautiful!

Whenever I was out with Bernie, we knew we didn't have to talk much. We found peace in our company and watching everything around us instead. We walked further along the path beside the stream of water that carried with it all the dirt and rotting leaves, making way for a new, bright life.

Gasp

I froze in panic. Bernadette's mouth dropped open in shock, as her hands flapped around in a tiny, happy dance. She always had to be dramatic. Her right hand waved around that much that she almost dropped her phone to the ground.

"Guess who's at Biddulph Moor Café?!" she asked, expecting me to somehow know.

Giving a blank expression, I shrugged my shoulders, waiting for Bernadette to answer her own question.

"Casey! He's just messaged me!" Her eyes lit up, like money had just dropped from the trees.

I remained quiet in her moment of excitement.

"You remember Casey, don't you April?"

Of course I remembered him. In fact, a little bit sparked inside me when hearing his name again for the first time in what felt like a decade, but I couldn't show that side to Bernadette.

"Aren't we heading to the café after this, anyway?" I asked.

"Yes! I'll let Casey know we're on our way and to stay put!"

I couldn't help but think Bernadette had planned this. I didn't ask, I never did, but a part of me feels as though she tried setting this up for me.

For the remainder of the walk, I noticed that Bernie had picked up her pace, so I followed suit so as not to fall back. It was also so I could see Casey again. I hadn't thought about him since that night. My mind has been so pre-occupied with working on myself that I never gave him a second thought, but hearing his name again sparked something I didn't know was there.

As we neared the café, I became nervous. I couldn't understand why, and I tried taking deep breaths through my nose to calm myself down. I found it increasingly difficult, as the harder I tried, the louder my breaths became. I couldn't let Bernie see that I was filled with nerves. I didn't need to give her a reason to think I wanted something. I stood a little further back from Bernadette so that she couldn't see me, as I pulled my hands from my pockets to notice I had uncontrollably started shaking and feeling clammy.

I hope the wind dries my hands… I hate this nervous disposition.

Moor café was a secluded yet delightful little cottage in the heart of Biddulph Moor. It was a thirty-minute walk from Biddulph Grange woods. Ivy grew up its walls and windows. Its old stonework portrayed many stories in its day and age. Carvings marked the walls from where past locals had once unintentionally signed their presence. The windows were fogged up from the warmth from inside.

Whenever I felt disquieted, I would often turn my

thoughts to that of Moor Café. Its history was everlasting and gracious. The café had once belonged to an elderly lady in 1958. She lived among these walls as her home. The fire would always burn, and her granddaughter would sit in the living room against the warmth, making different things for her grandmother, such as bags and jumpers.

In 1966, the elderly lady passed away. Her granddaughter (Monica) aged 22, retained the building for her own use. In 1970, the building went under construction to become what is now known as Moor Café.

Now, 73-year-old Monica carries on serving her regular customers alongside her son and granddaughter.

Upon first walking into the café with Bernie, her inquisitive look scanned the room for a familiar face. I, on the other hand, tried not to look. Keeping my head down, I removed my coat, trying to do little things to distract me from looking lost in a room full of eyes.

"Bernie, over here!" we heard from the corner of the room.

Casey sat upright, leaning out of an old, tatty armchair by the fire. My mind wandered into a world 50 years before now. A time when that same armchair sat a very different handsome man, taking a seat after a long day in the mines. The dirt and time had worn away the pattern and the olive-green velvet that wrapped around its cushioning. His arms waved, dragging me over with his current into the present. The colours from the flame in this dim room illuminated the shape of his defined jaw line. His dark hair was coiffed back, as though he was making an impression. His face looked clean shaven and moisturised, which is more than what I could say for his hands. Even in this dark room, my eyes adjusted to see calluses on the joints between each finger. His nails were cut short, probably to avoid dirt from sitting underneath.

As Bernadette brought me closer, I felt the lively fire burning against my delicate skin. The intense temperature change made my fingers and toes tingle, but it didn't stop me from moving away from the heat. To the wall on my right, I saw a framed black and white photo of Monica's grandma. The nostalgic atmosphere was all that I felt from the regular locals, who sat close by.

I rubbed my hands together hastily against the fire. The flames grew and roared against the chimney. The fire danced, displaying elegance and yet forms of ruthlessness. Looking deeper into the flames, I felt the heat engulf my thoughts and emotions. It relaxed certain obscure muscles at the nape of my neck. Any burdens I had felt were now less essential. Instead, the longer I looked into the prancing flames, the more my mind latched hold of other profound speculations: How are we here? I am in my favourite local café next to a man I barely know.

"Hello again, red," he said flirtatiously. *At least it was to me.*

"Hello, Anchorman," I responded humorously.

"I see my wise words stuck though, didn't they?"

Does he know I ended my relationship with Matthew?

I turned to Bernadette to see if she had a guilty look, but all I received as a response was shrugged shoulders and no words.

"Sorry, I just ordered myself a coffee. I wasn't sure how long you would both be."

"That's no problem, I can order a drink for me and Bernie."

"Thanks sweetie!" Bernadette squealed with a toothy smile. It was almost like the ecstatic face a toddler would pull when asking mum and dad for a treat.

"I'm just going to head to the toilet. April, could you order me a coffee with one sugar, please?"

I knew it. Leaving me on my own with Casey almost immediately when we get to the café. She planned this, didn't she?

The room fell silent for a moment. All I could hear was the fire crackling against the dry wood that burnt effortlessly. Strangely, it didn't feel awkward, but I did start to feel burnt as the heat from the fire became unbearable against the fair skin on my face. I sat back in my chair.

That's much more comfortable.

"I was surprised when Bernadette said you were nearby. I thought it would be best staying put for a while to see your face again."

I'm sorry, what? To see my face again?

This time it wasn't the fire burning up my skin, but my inner core temperature. This must have been a set-up, but right now, I didn't care. All I could think was that I need to control the redness in my face and hope that Bernie didn't come back too soon.

"Sorry," he apologised.

"Don't be sorry… I just wasn't expecting that comment." I recovered him from embarrassment.

Casey leaned forward in his armchair, edging closer to me. Now that he was closer, I saw not only the Jade green shade of his eyes that I saw at Bernadette's party, but a mix of colours that resembled a forest of green. The more I investigated them, the more mysterious he became. Just as it would be trying to look at a forest floor from a bird's-eye view above the large trees. I knew there was so much more going on underneath, but from above, I couldn't see it all, not yet.

"Red, I'll be honest with you. Since that night, I haven't been able to stop thinking about you. I don't know why and if you want me to stop talking, just say."

I started shaking my head slowly with my lips partially opened. I didn't realise at the time, but looking back, I suppose I couldn't have looked any more eager for the attention. It had felt like so long. To hear words like this sent trembles down my body, but finally they were trembles that resembled good sensation. The sort that you don't want to forget.

"What did I miss?" came an exhalation of words from behind my chair.

I couldn't take my eyes off Casey, but he gave me a wink to break the contact and focused his attention back on Bernadette.

"Sorry Bernie, I didn't get chance to go up and order," I expressed.

"Don't worry, I'll get them," Casey volunteered. "What would you both like?"

"Two coffees, both with one sugar, please."

"Milk?" he asked.

"Yes, but make sure the coffee is darker than my skin," I humorously added.

"That won't be difficult, red."

People had come in and out of the café more times than I could fully acknowledge, whilst the three of us continued into deep conversation. The staff would keep returning to us to keep the fire burning well and checking in on us. We ordered a couple of hot drinks, so we did not appear rude about using the space for a long period.

The back draft of the wind followed its way down the chimney, as I heard the fire fight against the wind with an almighty howl. All I kept thinking is how I would like to stay here all night and not have to leave to go back home on my own again.

We all felt the brisk cold when we left the warmth of the café to make our way outside. At times like this, it takes me back to the days when my grandparents would often tell me to remove my coat when inside the house, otherwise I will feel it even more when I go back outside. How right they were and yet I never seemed to learn. We weren't outside for long when the wind started forcing through my skin straight through to my bones. It hit that fiercely that it would take a full hot bath at Hell's temperature to make my body temperature stable again.

My cheeks began to feel like rubber, and I felt afraid to smile in fear that they would crack and bleed. Ironically, my ears and toes gave a burning sensation, as my body hastily acted against the weather. A tingling that would not surpass - Oh, how the irony could kill a person.

I looked down at my hands, that had evidently turned purple. I clenched my fists tightly, shoving them deep within my pockets. This did not help in the slightest, but the mentality told me that it was working to warm up my body temperature.

"Pub?" Casey asked.

Without hesitation, I nodded my head, possibly a little too enthusiastically. All I knew at this point was that I needed to get warm, and the pub was only across the road. Not only this, but to be able to stay out longer with friends meant that I didn't have to return to my empty home so soon.

My body shivered, ferociously. By reflex, I removed my hands from my pockets and intensely rubbed them together to bring back some kind of heat to my fingers.

"What do you drink, red?" Casey asked intently.

"Pink Gin and tonic," I responded immediately.

Casey tilted his head down, still looking at me before returning to the bar tender to make the order.

I reached into my bag, noticing very quickly my hands had turned from purple to red. It wasn't only my ears and toes that were burning and tingling now, but my face felt as though I had been sitting out in the sun for far too long. I tried searching for my purse to help pay for the drinks.

Cold fingertips gently brushed my hand, as Casey politely pushed me away from paying. He pulled some cash from his pocket to pay for the first round.

"I've got this." He looked back at me with a mischievous smirk appearing from behind his respectful act.

Bernadette grasped hold of my arm, scanning the room for a free table. Her heavy pull dragged me across to a little round table in the corner of the room. Casey juggled the glasses over to join us in this small area. I stroked the rim of the glass, watching each drip of condensation make its way to the base, soaking into the coaster below. Staring into the droplets, I began thinking about what would happen after this drink. How am I going to get home now? I left my car just down the road at my parents, but I won't be able to drive if I continue drinking.

I tried to reason with myself in silence, as Casey and Bernadette continued with the conversation between each other. I could always stop at my parents tonight, I reassured myself. That way I could drive home tomorrow. I still have a spare key to my parents, so I won't have to worry about waking them.

"Are you okay?" Bernadette asked. My eyes stopped blurring out the background, as I noticed I had absent-mindedly wiped away all the condensation from my glass, revealing only my finger marks around the bowl of my gin glass.

"Yes, sorry! In my own world." I laughed the moment away.

I tried to buy a round for us all that night, but Casey wouldn't allow it. He seemed to become merry very quickly and I was unsure if maybe he would regret all the payments in the morning.

As the night continued, I could see that Casey's attentiveness to his own actions had dropped. He would often fall into silence, staring at me, before returning to conversation. He knew that I could see what he was doing, and I chuckled a few times to myself. He responded to my giddiness with that sexy, but stern grin that could turn ice to water in a matter of seconds. The more he did this, the more I could see that Bernadette felt a little uncomfortable, but also too intrigued to leave… And so was I.

Between being in the pub finishing my gin and being stood in Casey's kitchen, I am unsure what had happened. I trippingly looked back to make out Bernadette passed out on Casey's sofa. I knew I wasn't spiked, but as usual, the alcohol told my brain that it was okay to sleep as it took control. Somehow, I ended up here, in this perfect cottage-style kitchen.

I regained focus, observing the oak kitchen units. He had farmhouse style hinges hanging on cupboard doors, dark granite worktops and a traditional AGA oven sat between, with a beautiful farmhouse green feature wall.

This is my kind of kitchen.

I returned to Casey who was leaning against the worktop, pointing me in the direction of a gin glass with his eyes.

"Another one for me?" I charmingly asked.

"As many as the lady desires," he seductively added to my comment.

Before I had a chance to move closer to my gin, Casey straightened himself. His chest became more pronounced, and I saw how some black chest hairs had appeared from under the buttons of his polo shirt. I examined his eyes again, but this time they were far different from before. His eyes became eager, as though they were looking straight through my navy-blue floral tunic. He managed to dig past my physical form and deeper, to the sound of my heartbeat drastically increasing.

He was now stood within a distance where I could feel his breath against my forehead, as he looked down at me, admiringly. I felt myself flush like I never have before. Have I felt this way before at the beginning of a relationship? It's been so long that the memory is only vague, but all I knew is that, in this moment, my mind felt melted from anything else I'd ever known. His eyes projected a new vision, different from the forest that I saw from above previously. Now I was on the forest floor, learning all its secrets, but I could still only see so far into the distance. I was now able to stand on the twigs and hear them crack and echo around the forest as birds flew from their nests in a stunned encounter. What else can I find down here? I wanted to find out.

He reached out, holding my arms in his hands. His fingers softly brushed my skin as I rolled back into silent bliss. The satisfaction didn't stop at my mind, as I felt the emotional and physical attentiveness rush through my body. I felt myself quake with the urge to collapse under his touch, but was this the alcohol or me? Am I just in wanting because I miss the feeling of being truly wanted?

Who cares?

My mind tried its best to block out any complications and to let these next few moments happen. He continued to brush his fingers lightly against my skin, while watching me take this time to approve the simplicity of his caring nature. Not only did the goosebumps rise, but I felt my nerve endings all come to the surface and tingle at the feeling of him being this close.

My heart was throbbing against my chest in a rhythmic, wanting passion. My heart over-ruled my mind, sending forward messages to the rest of my body. The warm, beating sensation in my chest transitioned as it travelled south. Imagine hitting a countryside hill in a car doing over 50 MPH. Can you recall that feeling in your stomach for a split second? That feeling stayed in my stomach, moving further down, transitioning back to a rhythmic throbbing sensation in my knickers. All senses had dissipated, leaving me in a submissive state.

"You're beautiful, red."

I smiled appreciatively, as I opened my eyes back to his. My bottom lip slightly parted, asking for him to lean in. He reciprocated this move, but to my own guilt I stepped back.

Why did I just do that?

"I'm sorry Casey. I'm still a little broken and we have both had too much to drink. I still barely know you."

He gave a shortened snort, but I could tell there was frustration behind his smile.

"Maybe so, red. I will respect that, but I'm not going anywhere anytime soon."

I watched as he picked up his phone from the worktop. He approached me again, much quicker this time, and gave a passing kiss on my forehead.

"Goodnight, red. I think Bernie is asleep on the sofa already, but it does pull out as a double sofa bed."

With that, he turned his back and made his way upstairs.

Why did I stop?

Hangover

    The wind was lost and confused. It changed the course of its direction through the trees surrounding us. The wind brushed past my hair in frustration, blowing it into my face. I fought back the red fog with my hands, holding my hair behind my ears.

    Twigs crunched beneath my bare feet as I continued walking forward. I couldn't look back, although it wasn't clear to me why. All I knew was that I needed to keep moving. The crunching stopped. I felt something soft brush beneath my feet. Glimpsing down, I saw white emerging from the wet ground.

    Kneeling down in my white, lacy, floral dress, the darkened soil moulded through my fingers. White egret orchids in bloom for miles and miles. Picking one from the ground, the flower sat in the palm of my hand. The orchid spread its petals further out to show a bird preparing for its first flight, but where would it go?

    My eyes squeezed shut as the wind ferociously forced itself against me. I held onto the ground with my hands holding on to nothing but soil to keep me in place. After a few seconds, the wind disappeared as quickly as it came back. I opened my eyes again and watched the white egret orchid flowers lift from their stems and disperse together, as though they were a murmuration of starlings flying in perfect formation. They began twisting and looping in unison, until every last one had left the ground, leaving a stag stood in the distance, watching the orchids dance with me. My focus turned from the white egret orchids to the stag. His eyes locked with mine in fear before turning away to run. I lifted my dress from the bottom to allow me to move quicker across the forest floor. I attempted to keep pace with the deer until water flooded from the skies above the trees. The faster I tried to run across the ground, the more my feet began to sink, slowing my movement and causing me to collapse into the earth. I looked up at the trees that had given into the weight of the rain through their leaves, each droplet of water falling on to my face. I closed my eyes and opened them for another time.

"Gross!" I exclaimed.

I pushed Bernie away from me as she drooled onto my face, but she was still fast asleep.

Light had started appearing through the drawn curtains into Casey's living room. I looked over at my phone to check the time. 10:03am.

"Shit!" I muttered to myself.

"Oh, you're awake?"

I heard a soft-spoken voice from another room. Peering over the arm of the sofa, I could see Casey stood in the kitchen, filling up the kettle in his dark shaded grey pyjama bottoms.

"Good morning," I hoarsely responded.

"I'll make us three some breakfast before taking you both home, if you like?"

There's no doubt about it. This man makes things flutter that I didn't even know existed and he isn't even doing anything in particular. I pondered on his words as he was working his way around the kitchen to make breakfast. *Do I have to go home so soon?*

I'll admit that I didn't like how last night had ended before going to sleep, yet he was pretending like it never happened. Maybe that way of thinking was probably for the best. It is so much easier to be able to draw the line in the sand and start again.

But he wanted to have sex with me. Why did I stop?

"What did I miss?"

I heard a gasp of air from behind as Bernie launched herself forward on the sofa. Her hair looked like a blonde matted mess. Her mascara had run down her cheeks, like coal being rubbed against a white fireplace hearth by a child who called it "*art*". I could tell that Bernie couldn't remember anything from last night, but saying that, I couldn't remember how we got here either...

"My memory is a bit vague, but how did me and Bernie end up back here, Casey?"

I heard him snort with laughter as he flipped the bacon in the frying pan. He looked back at me and Bernie, who remained silent, still awaiting an answer.

"Oh, you actually don't remember?" he inquisitively asked with one eyebrow raised.

I turned to Bernadette, shrugging my shoulders, before turning my head back with a silent and shameful shake.

Casey came over with the plates of food, handing us both a breakfast bap each. The silence remained for a few more moments, allowing the tension to grow.

"You both got a little bit out of hand to say the least," he opened with.

I could see the cogs trying to turn in Bernadette's mind, as she was biting down on her bottom lip and her cheeks began to flush, trying to remember. As for me, I was still none the wiser as to what happened last night, and I was in no mood to try to recall the past events now. I just sat waiting intently for Casey to explain.

"Oh… Oh no!" I watched as Bernie put her hands up to her mouth in utter disbelief.

Casey laughed at Bernie comprehending the events of last night.

"What? What happened?" I asked impatiently.

Casey looked at me teasingly with a smirk appearing on his face.

"I only went to the bar to get a refill for us all - two gins and a pint of lager. When I came back, Bernie had disappeared, so I asked April where she went."

"Oh no," Bernie interrupted the story.

"It seems you're both in a sibling rivalry when it comes to drinking games. I believe it started as a simple girl's truth or dare game, except you two decided to get personal by insulting each other."

I still had no recollection of last night, but I knew that Casey wasn't lying and the more I thought about what he said, the more panicked I became. What insults were we saying to each other? I knew that mine and Bernie's games can become very competitive and personal after a while. I thought it would be best not to ask Casey what was said. That way, I could pretend nothing happened. I can't say the same for Bernie, though. She pushed for answers like an officer questioning a potential witness at a crime scene.

"Casey, what did we say?" she demanded to know before letting the witness leave.

Casey laughed at our embarrassment before proceeding.

"I did wonder to myself why two friends would be so harsh to each other. April soon enlightened me that you two were like sisters and rather than bitching behind each other's backs, you would tell them to their face. Apparently after a few drinks, it becomes brutally honest."

I nodded my head, envisioning myself saying that the night before. There are too many groups of friends who will be nice to each other's faces, but behind closed doors, they'd disrespect their best friend to someone else. Both me and Bernie agreed we didn't want that kind of friendship, so we pledged to be honest with each other. Bernie soon became my non-biological sister. Someone I could entrust with anything and also put me in my place if I was making a wrong decision.

"I believe April had acne as a child." Casey chuckled to himself, trying not to look at me when he said it.

"Bernie! I thought it was meant to be a light-hearted game," I scorned her.

"This game was after a few drinks," she defended herself.

"Your insults were no lighter, April," Casey sided with Bernadette.

Bernie put her empty plate to one side as she leaned across, pulling my face into her chest and stroking my hair. My mouth was full as I tried to continue chewing with my face squashed against her right boob.

"You know I love you, Appy," she comforted me.

***

It felt like a parent dropping his kids off at school when Casey unlocked his car to drop me and Bernie off at home. Bernadette called dibs on the front passenger seat as I hopped into the back seat of his Land Rover. Bernadette could have walked to her house from Casey's, but I was positive she wanted to spend a little more time with me and Casey. I could tell by her expressions alone she wanted to see if anything developed and, to be truthful to myself, I also wanted to see if anything further would develop. I wanted it to.

"Is anything happening with you two?" Bernie broke the silence.

I could feel myself flushing again – The ginger curse!

"Not from what I can gather, Bernie," he disappointingly answered for the both of us.

Those few words struck me like sad chords being played on a piano. I stayed silent for the both of us at that time. I kept my head down, looking at my hands, trying to look anywhere but at Casey or Bernadette. Even though Bernadette only lived a short drive away, the journey seemed endless. I could tell everyone was probably trying to think of something to say to hide the awkwardness.

Finally, we're at Bernadette's.

"Thank you for letting us stop the night, Casey. I probably wouldn't have even been able to make it through my own door last night."

Bernadette twisted her head back like an owl, her eyebrows raised to me. "April, as always, I love you and I'll message you later tonight." She leaned over the front seat to give me a hug goodbye as she whispered in my ear, "I'll text you."

She shut the door, leaving me and Casey alone. Now I felt my stomach churn with emotion, or was this feeling the dire need to go to the toilet? My stomach always felt worse after being in nervous situations.

"You'll have to direct me to wherever you need to go, red," he said calmly.

"I just need dropping off at my parents," I added.

I directed him down the roads in Biddulph Moor, which luckily gave distraction from having a deep conversation. I looked up at the rear-view mirror in an attempt to see his face and perceive how he may be feeling from his facial expressions. His eyes were narrowed, and I tried to understand if he was frustrated with me, trying to think of conversation or perhaps just concentrating on the road ahead. His eyes took a glimpse at the mirror, catching my intense look into his.

Damn it!

I pulled away in embarrassment, but it was too late. He smiled back at me, his eyes giving a soft glow. I snickered at the thought of my own humiliation, but he remained silent with his smile still pushing all the right buttons. For the rest of that drive back, the smile did not fade.

He pulled up outside of the private lane, which led straight down to my parents' house. I could see my Golf sat looking back at me from the drive.

"What a beautiful car," he said admiringly.

"Thank you, she's mine," I said with pride in my voice.

"Shut up!?" he exclaimed in disbelief. His head turned around quicker than a Barn Owl spotting food in a wide-open field.

I relaxed back into my seat, nodding my head to him. Casey didn't move and didn't say another word for a few moments. Instead, we sat there looking at each other affectionately. This silence was better. It didn't feel uncomfortable. His bottom lip became slightly ajar, hesitating to say the next sentence. He thought about his words carefully, before regretting it.

"I'm sorry about last night," he said, while gently stroking the centre console of his car with his index finger. He looked up at me again for reassurance.

"Cards on the table, red… I knew you were unique from the first night I met you and I don't want this to just end. I made a mistake last night by being too forward… If you would let me, I'd really like to see you again." His eyes looked meaningful. A hint of hazel brown surrounded his pupils, just like the vision of the stag surrounded by forest green.

"I'd like that too," I responded in the giddiest tone a girl could do.

I reached into my handbag to find an old letter. I ripped a corner of the paper and began writing my number on it before passing it over to him. I gently stroked the palm of his hand as I pulled away with mine.

"See you again soon, Casey," I gently promised to him, as I jumped out of the back of his car. I waved back to him, but he didn't leave. It wasn't until I was nearing my parents' house that I looked back and noticed he was waiting to ensure I safely got inside the house.

What a gentleman...

I made it to the front door of my parent's house, before I turned back around again. He was still sat there. I watched as he waved to me and drove off.

Flowers say a lot

I stared at myself in the mirror of my bedroom. The blue colouration from my eyes became brighter, as the sunlight from the window glared in and reflected from the mirror's surface. I could almost see the ocean waves crashing against the wind. When I looked closer, I tried to see below the surface of the waves, but everything was dark and unknown to the upside world. I tried swimming further down, but I could not withstand the pressure before having to return to the surface.

I was trying so hard to understand what was going on beneath the surface of me, but to no avail. I was struggling to understand the emotions that were building up in my mind, causing me to feel warm, tingly sensations. It is difficult to explain what women experience. For a man, it is so easy. If you like someone, all the blood rushes to one area and poof! Your friend says hello! I'm sure if a man was to read this, we would be in a long dispute. However, how many men have expressed needing an emotional connection to be able to perform? They only need a single image. Why do you think sperm banks only need a magazine and a pot?

As a woman, so much more is to be experienced. With more feelings, come more complications for satisfaction. As difficult as that may sound, that is where the fun begins. If you like the easy life, you probably shouldn't date women. To be with a woman means learning their puzzles and what pleases them. So many relationships would thrive, if only they both took the time to learn about each other inside and out. Some puzzle pieces may not fit together to begin with, but if you take a moment to stand back and look at what you have, a perfect picture may begin to form.

Physical touch doesn't even poke at the threshold of how to please a woman. The first and most important step is to build an emotional connection with that person. This doesn't even have to be anything difficult. An emotional connection can be built almost instantly through admiration or pride for something they have done. Showing interest in a hobby, assisting where help is needed, or heartfelt conversation is a great place to start.

Just the emotional sense of being wanted is enough to make a woman physically melt into euphoria. It is as though Cupid is consumed by emotion and shoots his arrow further south, away from the heart. Once the arrow hits, the feelings do not succumb to one area, but spread throughout the body. It starts by increasing blood flow to the salivary glands, creating an increased amount of saliva or as more commonly known as *literally* drooling over someone you're attracted to. Next, the arrow's poison travels further down to your heart. It feels as though your heart is pounding against your chest as the blood flow increases around your body. Breathing becomes increased with a sense of emotional ecstasy as your body begins wanting more. It doesn't stop there, though; Mr Cupid's arrow will make its way to your stomach. Imagine someone traces their fingers tips along the inside of your elbow, then transfer that feeling to your stomach. That tingling sensation works its way further south to the pinnacle point. The tingling then changes to a throbbing sensation. This throbbing causes you to cross your legs and fidget with anticipation and want. This poison spreads through a woman's body quicker than the bite of a King Cobra and yet all of this can be created just from emotional connection alone!

Next comes *the tease*. The feeling of being so close to having it all, but something holds you back in a wanting passion. Again, teasing doesn't have to refer to bondage, masks and tools. This can be caused just by giving the right look. The look that says "I want you, but you can't have me, not yet…" A built-up temptation that is difficult not to break.

This was the stage I'd reached, being left to want it so badly, but knowing I couldn't have it all just yet. That was my fault. I brought stage three to a stop out of my own principle. I was teased with a potential to lead to stage three, but I said *no*. Now, I let gravity pull me back, so that I collapsed onto my bed. I closed my eyes for a moment, seeing visions of red reflecting from the sunlight. Images started forming and my mind wandered back to Casey holding my arms. Yes, back to stage two, the tease! Something simple, like the gesture of holding my arms, but that simple gesture meant something more, much more. My mind now went into an imaginary stage three, or what is more commonly known as *fantasy land*.

I smiled to myself as my mind created various scenarios. I felt my body twisting and my legs crossed over as I tensed with arousal. That was until I felt something vibrating in my right hand. I looked over to see a text from an unknown mobile:

Unknown: Hey red, it's Casey! I just thought that I should be the first to let you know, I have made yet another mistake trying to make up for the first time I made a

mistake… So, I may have bought some flowers to say sorry for the forward move I made last night. Don't thank me yet though. I may have knocked on the same house I dropped you off at earlier, thinking you lived there with your parents. Turns out you don't, and your parents awkwardly explained that to me… Anyway, your parents have the flowers to pass on to you, from me. Your parents also might have a few questions too. I AM SO SORRY!

Well, shit!

I felt as though I was a child experiencing a sugar crash. I was ecstatic in my own world and in moments that has been taken away. My heart was still beating just as fast, but this was no longer a euphoric feeling, but a sense of panic. I stayed silent, staring at the home screen of my phone. All I expected was for my parents to ring any moment, bombarding me with questions that not even I knew the answer to.

Wait… Why would he take flowers there? He knows that my parents are there regardless of whether I live with them or not. Why would he risk taking them there? Is he being too forward? Is this the red flag that I warned myself to stay away from?

Minutes must have passed by, with my phone still in my hands, awaiting a call. I was in complete shock, not knowing what to do. I shook my head to gather some sense of the situation.

That's it! I'm calling him. I need him to understand that this is too much.

I unlocked my phone and hovered my thumb over the call icon.

Stop hesitating. Just do it, April.

I put the phone up to my ear as I heard it dial out. I suddenly felt like I had a social anxiety disorder. My mind had gone blank. I really should have thought about what to say before I rang him.

"Hello?"

I stayed in a silent fear, not able to talk. My bottom lip kept stammering, in an attempt to make a noise, but I didn't know how.

"April, are you there?"

"Hey! Sorry, I'm here…" I finally answered.

"Are you alright?"

This is it. I need to tell him.

"No, not really…"

"Talk to me, please. You're starting to worry me," Casey pleaded.

"Casey, I know you didn't mean any wrong by it, but why would you think bringing flowers to my parent's house would be a good idea?"

"I'm sorry…" He sounded genuinely guilty and upset by this. Probably more by my tone.

"When I dropped you off yesterday, I assumed you still live with your parents. I wanted to right my wrongs from the day before and I thought it would be a nice gesture…"

The call fell silent as I tried to control my anger. I knew he didn't mean any wrong by it and if I worded this the wrong way, I may never hear from him again.

"Regardless of me living there or not, did you really think it would be a good idea to bring something as romantic as flowers to my parent's house when I've only met you twice beforehand?"

"I'm sorry, I wasn't thinking straight. I do care about you a lot, April. I know we still have so much to learn about each other, but I want to learn more," Casey said.

"Casey, I'm not angry, but you have to realise that this is too much. It is a lovely gesture and under different circumstances, I would be ecstatic but…"

Casey made a sound like trying to stifle laughter.

Why is he laughing? I'm trying to have a serious conversation over this and he's laughing?

"I'm sorry, what's so funny?"

"Sorry, I just can't carry on anymore…"

He's laughing, again!

I could feel myself become angrier. Is he patronising me? Why is this now turning around to make me feel like the idiot?

"Can't carry on with what anymore, Casey?!" I said testily.

"I didn't take any flowers to your parent's house today," he confessed.

I didn't respond. How could I? None of this was making any sense. I didn't even want to respond, I just wanted him to be straight with me, rather than taking all the back roads to get to the main story. My face heated, and I could feel my hand tighten around my phone.

"It was a fun test!"

"Test?! Fun?! How is *this* any of those things?" I said.

"Yeah," Casey sighed. "I'm starting to regret starting a conversation with you this way."

"And I'm starting to regret giving you my number..."

"Sorry, I should have just gone with the usual *"Hey, how are you?"* type conversation."

I sighed to myself, with my head shaking in one hand and my phone pulled away from my ear. I heard Casey break the silence again with a nervous cough to gain my attention. I needed to listen to what he had to say.

"My intention was to throw in a scenario to get to know you better, red... See, I knew that this scenario would throw you off guard and your reaction to it would tell me a lot about the person you are really. I never did visit your parents' house or take any flowers, for that matter. Your reaction could have gone one of three ways: If you were happy, that would tell me that you're the type of person to jump into a relationship without giving it a second thought. If you stayed silent, or avoided the topic when we next spoke, that would mean you keep your feelings hidden away, without wanting to communicate or resolve. The last one would be to contact me to be able to understand why I have done it and to give a chance for reasoning."

I thought about what he had said in silence for a few moments. I didn't know if I felt angry or impressed. I had never had a man play a game to understand a woman's intentions. Could this be because he has had relationship issues before? Was he wanting to test the waters for red flags before he decided to take the next step with me?

All I could think was that he had put thought into this. He'd probably been sat at home, the same as me, thinking about us and all the potentials. Maybe concerns crossed his mind and this was his way of finding out more?

Does this mean I passed his little test?

But I don't want to be some kind of test to him…

"There's four ways," I said.

"What?"

"There's four ways in which I could have reacted, not three. What if I decided to ring my parents first?"

"Ah! Well, I ruled that option out already," he said.

"Why?"

"You've already proven to me that you're afraid to bring things to their attention, in fear that they will be disappointed in you," he said confidently.

Does he think he's Sherlock? He must have studied psychology or something.

I was out of my comfort zone. I felt like he could have told me my whole life story and why I was the way I was from my childhood.

"I'm sorry Casey, but how could you possibly know that?"

"The way you looked around for your parents when I dropped you off. Without even realising you were doing it, you crouched further down in the seat in case anyone was around to see. I wasn't ashamed by it, but I could tell straight away that you were afraid of confrontation."

Yep! He's Sherlock… One thing's for sure, I am not going into a life of crime because he will sniff it out like a wolfhound.

"OK, Mr Holmes. You've had your fun. Now it's my turn to get to know you, but not like this. I am free next weekend if you are?"

"Leave the planning to me. Let me know your address and I will come to pick you up once I've made the arrangements," Casey said, a smile in his voice.

"It's a date." I grinned.

"I look forward to it."

"Oh, but Casey…" I said, a warning note to my voice. "Never and I mean *never* do that to me again."

***

I struggled to sleep that night. I tossed and turned until my duvet cover had finally broken free from me, falling to the floor. I wrestled with my mind for hours to try to understand Casey, but the more I tried to understand, the more confused I became. It has always been a problem for me, trying to sleep with unanswered questions.

I just need to remember not to become love blind. I can't let this feeling of attraction and affection affect my instinct to identify the red flags that I have been succumbed to in the past.

Remember ASCENT, April. Don't forget it.

I finally managed to drift off into a sleep when I made an agreement with my mind to call on Bernadette the following morning to discuss my feelings with her. I knew Bernadette couldn't help with all the answers I needed, but ever since first knowing her, she has provided moral support. That's all I needed for that moment.

First Date

"He said what?" Bernadette shouted from the kitchen, as I explained Casey's bizarre and unnerving test.

"You heard it right," I confirmed.

The living room smelled delicious, as Bernie set about making pancakes for the two of us. I lay down on her sofa, making myself at home, as I knew she needed this time to process what the hell had happened to me. It was always cosy in Bernie's home. It was small, but she made the most of the space she had, literally transitioning this house to a home.

Her living room presented shades of admiral blue and mustard yellow. I tucked the velvet bumble bee sofa cushion behind my head and closed my eyes momentarily, in an attempt to re-energise from an awful night's sleep.

Bernadette had always been able to give sound advice, no matter what the situation was. Whether it was something she had experienced herself or not, she always seemed to know the right words to say to comfort me, and this was one of those times.

"He is clearly intrigued by you, April. The fact he has admitted that he watches your every move to try to decipher your thoughts and intentions can only mean that he wants to learn about you. It's just down to you now and whether you let him in to learn more, or if you want to hide those intentions from him."

Hide my intentions? Can she see through me too? Does she know about my potential intentions?

So many questions flicked through my mind from her response, but I became easily distracted when a plate of food was placed in front of me. I shovelled in as much pancake as could physically fit into my mouth. I could see from the corner of my eye that Bernadette was looking at me with disgust.

With an open mouth, I confessed, "This is what you call a mouthgasm."

My phone flashed on the coffee table and before I had a chance to place my plate down, Bernie was already snooping.

"Casey!" She looked at me ecstatically.

I grabbed hold of my phone. I chose not to unlock it, but to view the text from my notifications bar so that he didn't see that I had read it already.

Casey: First date is organised! I will pick you up on Saturday at 6pm. Make sure you're wearing a modest dress.

Very demanding...

"What does it say?" Bernadette enquired.

I turned to see a child sat cross-legged and quiet, waiting for the teacher to give out awards for the deserving pupils. I unlocked my phone, showing her the text. She lowered the phone so I could see her thrilled eyes peering above the screen. I could see that the inner child still hadn't left her.

"I've never seen this side to Casey before, it's quite exhilarating," she chuckled.

Is it only me that sees another side to this message? Someone who is controlling over a situation and doesn't provide the full picture? Or am I just emotionally troubled from my previous relationship and now I see the negative in everything? Again, I have so many questions to ask myself, but no real answers.

April: It's a date.

I responded maybe a little too quickly. I need to find out for myself and answer my own questions. It is still too early for me to call judgement, but I need to stay cautious. Now I just need a modest dress.

***

I sat cross-legged on the wet soil that soaked into my white dress. I could feel myself sinking further into the mud below, but I couldn't move. I no longer struggled to escape. Two long, skinny legs stood in front of me above the mud, but they did not sink like me. I gazed up with the sun beaming down on my vision, making it difficult to see the figure. Its head lowered, shadowing the sun. A white egret stood face to face with me. It lowered its beak to the mud and rested its head against mine. It was eerily quiet. The wind did not howl, the birds did not call out, the leaves and twigs covering the ground did not rustle.

The mud had now consumed me to my breasts, as I took deep breaths, knowing that they were my last. I lifted my hand up to the white egret. It stretched its wings out as far as they could span before taking flight. I held my last breath as the egret flew off into the sun. It dispersed into hundreds of orchids around my consumed body. A white egret orchid landed in the palm of my hand. I clenched it, as I dragged it into the depths with me.

I woke up in my own bed breathing heavily. Dropping my body back down to my mattress, I felt a wet patch against the side of my face. After leaning up to look, I noticed a patch of sweat from where I had struggled emotionally in my sleep. I pulled a disgusted face at my sheets before going to wash my face in the bathroom sink. I rubbed my eyes with the water before coming face to face with my hand-held mirror on the windowsill. How could anybody admire this? The blue oceanic eyes, surrounded by nothing but darkness from restless nights.

The day stayed bright, as I looked out of my bedroom window at my Golf, crying out for attention on the side of the street. I had no responsibilities, but my own. Sometimes I struggled to keep myself motivated to tick off all my own responsibilities. I threw on my overalls from the bottom of my wardrobe and looked at myself in the floor-standing mirror.

Yes, you're definitely an eye-catcher, April!

I rolled my eyes at my reflection.

As much as I hated the maintenance on Gordon, it kept my mind occupied from dwelling on personal troubles. I lay a large piece of cardboard underneath Gordon, like a parent placing a mat down to change a baby's dirty nappy. Time to wipe the dirty arches with some sandpaper before putting a clean pair of nappies back on. Is this what my life has come to? My only mothering responsibility is to a car?

What a life!

I scrubbed away at the rust. Luckily, it was only surface rust, so I saved Gordon just in time from dreaded holes. I pinged open the tin of Hammerite with a flat head screwdriver, before putting on a coat to the arches. Now I wait for it to dry.

"Good morning!" the postman called as he skipped down my drive.

"Good morning! More bills?" I answered.

He passed over the letters to me. Without looking, I disregarded them to the doorstep beside me.

"Lovely looking car you've got there," he added, trying to make small talk.

"Yes! Definitely a pain in the arse to keep on top of though."

He chuckled, before asking, "Would you ever consider selling?"

"Gordon? No. He's been with me since the beginning and I have put in so much time, it would be a shame to sell."

"Well, if the time ever does come, let me know," he requested, as he left to the next address.

I shook my head, since I had never been asked if I would consider selling before. A Golf MK1 was the first and only car I ever wanted. I was never sure what exactly captured my interest apart from one summer day I went to a vintage car show and saw a 1977 drop top Golf MK1. The Golf was black all over, apart from a red stripe which followed around the grill. The silver BBS wheels made it impossible to stare at when the sun reflected off them. I recall the owner asking if I wanted to sit in with my mum and, of course, I jumped at the opportunity. As a young girl, I felt like a racer in that car, and it filled me with such a thrill. When I bought Gordon, it gave me that nostalgic feeling that I never wanted to let go of, and to this day, I don't want to let go.

I smiled back at Gordon, as if he had his own human emotions. That's all I could do for the moment anyway until the Hammerite dries. I wiped my hands down the sides of my overalls. The red Hammerite added to the collection of dirt and rust that also covered every inch of my body.

As soon as I walked through my front door, I stripped down out of my clothes, so I didn't tread dirt through the house, and ventured upstairs to the bathroom. I began running the hot water into the bath, before fighting with a hair bobble to let my hair drop loose again.

You scruffy looking ginger!

I dipped my toe in the water gently to absorb and adjust to the temperature. The hairs on my legs and arms stood out as far as they could reach, giving me a similar feeling to that of goosebumps at a concert. I sat down in the water, holding my legs close to my chin. I didn't move for a few moments, as I allowed the hot water to engulf my negative aroma and allow them to disperse along with the dirt on my body.

Hello again, razor!

As much as I hated the time it takes to shave my body, it did make me feel good about myself after. The feeling of moving your hand over your leg and knowing it's smooth… for a day or two, anyway. After applying oils, I felt happy with myself for the first time in what seemed like a lifetime.

I wandered around the house trying to find something to wear. I needed a *modest* dress. Modest… That crossed out any of my clubbing dresses. Not that one, it's too booby. Nope! Not that one, it's too short. Does it have to be a dress? I pushed through my wardrobe full of clothes like a woman fighting with others on a 50% sale rail in a high-end store. That's when I stopped at an old knee-length, green skater dress. I carefully tried on the dress to make sure it still fit, and I felt elated to see that it fit perfectly around my figure. I twirled around in a circle to see the dress flare out at the bottom like a dancing ballerina doll. I tightened the bow around my waist as I smiled at myself in the mirror.

Hopefully he won't realise that this is an old dress…

I twisted my hair up, indecisive whether to have my hair in a clip or not. Twisting my head from side to side, I chose to have the clip to show the jewellery around my face. I smirked again at myself. It's not often that I feel good about myself anymore.

My phone vibrated on the top of drawers as I looked to see a text from Casey. My smile widened in acknowledgment.

Casey: What's your address?

I forgot he only has my parents' address.

April: 97 Peregrine Drive, Mow Cop.

When I heard the knock at my door, I could feel the nerves build up as quickly as the feeling of shock running through your arms and hands when holding onto an electric fence. I tried to remain confident as I brushed down the bottom of my dress, inhaling and exhaling deeply.

You look amazing and you're ready, April.

I took one step at a time in my heels as I steadied myself downstairs. The feeling of nostalgia engulfed me, taking me back to prom night, when my parents stood at the bottom of the stair to record the moment as a memory. This time there was no one there to cheer me on or to save this memory for me. It's just me this time and I can do it. I am the strong, independent woman that I keep trying to tell myself I am.

One last deep breath before opening that door.

He stood there in a navy-blue suit and white slim fit shirt that exposed all his best features. His chest was prominent, and I could tell that his stomach was toned beneath the tucked in shirt. His dark hair coiffed back and his sharp jawbone on show after a fresh shave. His face looked soft, and I wanted to touch it to see if it felt just as it looked. I hated to think of how gormless I must have looked in that moment as I drooled over this man standing in my doorway.

I was so torn away from being in the moment and, instead, stayed in my dream state that I failed to notice his reaction towards me. The green of his eyes wavered above me, like looking up at the Northern Lights in the atmosphere. The glowing green gave me an electric pulse of energy, passed down from the aurora borealis. In an instant, aurora borealis tried fighting against the clouded rain as his eyes began watering. I could see Casey trying to fight it back, but seeing his emotion come out in the open just showed me how human he really was. His bottom lip was slightly parted and the more we stared at each other, the more I noticed his hands fidgeting for anything close by. He clenched his fists and stretched his fingers out again repetitively. He opened one hand in a relaxed position before slowly raising it to my cheek and stroking softly. I nudged my face closer into his hand, accepting his physical approach.

"You look radiant, Miss…"

He stared at me blankly, as we both came to the realisation that we never actually knew each other's last names.

"Miss Jones and you are Mr?"

"Mr Woods," he confirmed.

He held out his arm for me to link as he walked me to his car. As a gentleman would, he opened the passenger side door for me to sit in.

I wonder how long this lasts before he stops with the gentlemanly gestures.

We were driving for almost an hour before I worked up the words to ask him where we were going to. He chuckled to me as he glanced across, giving me one last look with a smile on his face.

"Not long now, red," he evasively confirmed.

I kept my legs crossed tightly and my arms close to my side so that I did not come across as too promising, or even misleading, too soon. I kept my eyes focused outside my window as I kept looking out for road signs to give me an indication of the destination. I knew we were in the Peak District, but with so many lovely little villages and towns around, it was difficult to determine where he would be stopping. With darkness setting in early, I became visually impaired to our surroundings.

Bakewell! - I do love it here. Good choice, Mr Woods.

Casey quickly jumped out of the car to assist me out of the passenger side. I held onto his hand as I steadied myself to a standing position. The sound of the river to our side filled me with a calming consciousness. I closed my eyes for a brief moment to listen to the river in harmony, before opening my eyes to see Casey stood there admiringly with his arm reached out for me to join him again.

Eclipse was the name of the restaurant that we had our first date, and I will always remember the dimmed lights in the room. Some of the wall lights had a darkened covering on the face with led lights behind, giving the *eclipse* feeling to the room. Each table was carefully prepared for guests with placemats that reminded me of the texture of the moon. In the centre of each table was a vase containing different types of yellow flower, thus resembling the sun light.

"A table has been booked for Mr Woods."

"Yes, this way please, Mr Woods." The waitress brought us to our table, providing a food and wine menu for the two of us, as we sat surrounding the yellow marigold flowers in the centre of the table.

"So, what do you think?" Casey asked, full of eager and happy abundance about him.

"I am very impressed thus far, Mr Woods," I replied with a menu covering my mouth from his vision. In reality, I was not used to somewhere as fancy as this and I felt out of place.

I can't show him that, though.

I looked down at the menus, panicking. What do some of these even mean? Which wine is best? How much can I spend? Will we be splitting the bill?

Look for something familiar, April.

"Can I interest you both in still or sparkling water?" I heard a voice behind me ask.

"Still water, please," Casey managed to respond for both of us, as I was still in deep turmoil trying to decipher the menu.

"Are you ready to order?" The waiter further asked.

"I believe so…" Casey looked at me for confirmation before returning to the waiter.

"Yes! Yeah, sorry," I stumbled with my words.

"And what would the lady like for starters?"

Quickly April! Name something you recognise!

"Could I have the pâté en crew… No, Crow… Sorry"

"Pâté en croûte, please," Casey humbly corrected me whilst stroking my hand for reassurance.

I didn't even hear what Casey ordered for himself, as my mind was repeating the moment of embarrassment over and over in my head.

A time which will haunt me while I try to sleep at night…

Our waiter had brought out three separate dishes each and a glass *or two* of wine for me that Casey had ordered. The evening was full of conversation and laughter, although I wasn't sure if it was the wine interpreting my speech, or if it was Casey being able to bring out the actual me. The me that is confident when stood behind a mirror by myself without outside influences. The woman that knows exactly what she wants, without somebody chirping down her ear.

The waiter cleared up our table before asking if we would like anything else. Casey looked at me with another genuine smile. I responded slowly, shaking my head from side to side, while exhaling to show I was full. Casey looked at the waiter and requested the bill. As soon as the waiter left to print off the bill, I turned to Casey.

"Would you like me to help with the bill?" Before he had a chance to answer, I reached my hand across the table for my purse to get my card. Casey placed his hand over mine, restricting its movement.

"Don't be so silly, red. You can clean the dishes in the kitchen for payment," he joked.

I laughed hysterically. It wasn't that funny, but I knew the wine was coming out now.

After paying the bill, Casey stretched out his hand this time to ask for mine as we walked outside. I started heading towards his car in the car park, when I felt a tug pulling me to one side.

"I thought we could have a walk by the river before heading home, if that's OK?"

I nodded my head with a giddy grin as we followed a footpath by the side of the river. The sky was clear, with a crescent moon making an appearance. Its partial white glow shimmered down on the water to our left. I noticed a path where people had ventured off down the trodden grass to the riverbank. I ran off in front to go down to the river's edge, as Casey tried to keep close behind. The water looked calm and entrancing, encouraging me to go in. I began removing my heels with haste to paddle at the river's edge.

"Not skinny dipping on a first date, are you, red?" I could tell Casey said it jokingly, but his face looked unsure. I winked at him without saying a word, turning my back to him, chasing the wind into the river's current.

"It's cold!" I shrieked.

Casey laughed as he began untying the laces of his shoes. I watched him carefully as he groaned, kneeling down.

"Are you OK?" I apprehensively asked.

"All good, just a little knee pain from work," he clarified.

I flicked some water up at him with my toe in a playful fashion.

"You're in for it now, red," he warned me as he rolled his suit trousers up on his muscly calves, chasing me into the water. He cupped the clear water in his hands before throwing it up in the direction of my face. I screamed as though I wasn't expecting it. I closed my eyes, hoping, no praying, that the mascara wouldn't start running down my face, making me look like a raccoon. I felt his hand cup the underside of my chin, bringing my face up to meet his. I giggled, looking at all his features, taking in everything from that exact moment. Everything fell silent in an instant. It was as if the waters stopping flowing and the wind stopped singing through the tree leaves. He leaned in closer, and I felt his lips around mine. I reciprocated and melted in his arms.

"Come on," he said promisingly.

"Where are we going?" I nervously enquired.

"I recall you once said at a party that you have never had sex outside, Miss Jones."

Oh my…

He grabbed hold of my hand, leading me to a grass verge where bushes and trees shielded us. Casey pulled me close to him by my waist. His other hand tucked my hair behind my ear. He looked admiringly down at me once more, before burying his face into my neck.

I groaned at the unexpected rush running through my body all at once. I gasped and flicked my head from side to side to look for anyone around. Casey started kissing up to my lips, where his eyes met mine.

"Stop panicking, no one can see us, trust me."

I let myself melt in defeat within his arms as he continued kissing down my chest. I felt his hand slowly lower below the hem of my dress, then he lifted it up over my head and threw it to the ground. He stood back in amazement at me. I began twisting and turning with nerves, trying to cover my breasts with my arms and I crossed my legs in an attempt to hide myself.

"You are beautiful, April Jones," he breathlessly admitted to me.

He brought himself in closer again, so that I could feel his breath against my forehead. He lifted my chin with his finger as he stared down and kissed me harder than before. My whole body was tingling and my weight collapsed into his arms. He lifted me up around his waist and lowered my back onto the soft, dry grass.

I watched as he sucked air in through his teeth, as if trying to fight back pain.

"Are you okay?" I anxiously questioned him.

"Don't worry, I think I just knocked my bad knee against a rock or something. I'm fine!"

He lifted my arms above my head to restrain me with one hand, while the other hand trailed down the figure of my body. My hair fell over my cheeks, and I closed my eyes into a sexual fantasy that had come to life. His fingers caressed my shoulder, slowly but gently, moving further up along my neck. I cocked my head to the left, feeling the cold grass brush against my face. His warm gentle fingers made the hairs on my arms stand up straight, encouraging every part of my body to be pulled towards him.

I wonder what is going through his mind...

The light from moonlit sky provided a slight visual of his pronounced features, making it unbearable for me to hold back from touching him. His eyes glared knowingly into mine, but yet with all of this knowing and admiration, there was still a sense of wonder. Our lips were apart, and our breathing became heavy with anticipation. Our eyes remained staring, yet not a single word had been said. Words didn't need to be spoken in moments like this.

These were only moments of gentleness, as he reached down, pulling me up towards him to kiss me harder and more persistently. I reciprocated the wanting passion, placing my hands around his face, and he likewise placed his hands around mine.

A sensation flooded the lower part of me, making me feel a warm wetness between my legs, in contrast to the cold water that had immersed my lower legs from the river. This warm sensation had been building for some time, wanting to be released, wanting him!

I pushed him back so that he lost his balance and fell to the ground, with his arms by his sides, keeping him upright. I climbed onto his lap, my legs on either side, allowing him to move his hands precariously on my arched back, feeling every curve. He stopped as soon as he reached my lower back. The slow but gentle rubs that wound me up, leaving me wanting more without hesitation. I wanted rougher, so I kissed harder to entice the throbbing between my legs. He slowly pulled one hand back as I continued kissing him.

Slap I groaned, hard! His right-hand hit against me.

More! I want more!

I began rotating my hips in a rhythmic motion on top of his cock, as I felt it push against me. Again, he slapped me harder that time. I felt myself drip more with excitement. I moan his name, as though I was worshipping him. I wanted it and Casey knew that, but he wanted me to play along with his little teasing game.

He slapped me harder again as he amused himself at my enjoyment and pleading. I looked down at him once more, smirking in complete silence. His laughing had come to a stop and in exchange, I watched as his eyes moved from side to side, absorbing every little detail about me.

I felt his arms move around my legs again, as he lifted me back up with a groan and lay me back down in the grass. From beneath his shirt hung a chain with a little charm on. It looked handmade and in the shape of an anchor. I lifted my hand up to feel the rough edges of the metal anchor that hung from his neck.

"That's cute!" I whispered in an intriguing tone, wanting to know more.

He didn't respond to me, but rather tucked his chain back beneath his shirt and away from my view. For a moment, I wondered if I had brought up a story that was too early to be told just yet, but Casey made sure it would escape from my mind almost immediately, as he bit down onto my lip. I rolled my eyes back and began stretching my body and arching myself to allow him full control to move me as he wished.

With two fingers, he pulled my knickers down towards my ankles and his head followed down, until he reached *there*. He began kissing slowly and gently around, causing me to become impatient. I tried to fight against him by lifting and moving my hips so he would kiss the spot I wanted, but he held me down harder, restraining me with just his hands.

"If you keep moving, I'll keep you wanting longer," he warned.

I tried to hold myself back, but the harder I tried, the more I moaned. His soft, warm, wet tongue gently kissed my clitoris, and I stretched back to finally be able to release. I lifted my hand above my head, grasping hold of the grass in my grip. I looked down at him, seeing his dark hair shimmering in the moonlight. I brushed my other hand through his hair, grabbing hold of it. His rhythm had changed from gentle to passionate within minutes. I felt a finger move up the inside of my legs. The wetness of myself against his finger felt pleasing, as he lightly moved in a circular motion around my vulva. He slid his middle finger inside so that only the tip was in, as he continued licking back and forth. I screamed whilst grabbing hold of his hair harder. He synchronised the movement of his finger, moving in and out of me, in time with his tongue. His middle finger gradually moved further inside me, bending at the tip so he could hit the g spot.

"That's it, there!" I screamed.

He pulled his finger out.

No, please no! Don't stop.

I looked down again, biting my lip with irritation. I watched as he sucked his middle finger and then returned to push two fingers inside, deep and hard. My head knocked back and my eyes rolled into the back of my head. I clutched at anything around me with my hands, as I could feel each part of myself in an unknown pleasure.

Each time he hit against my g spot; I felt a sense of build-up like no other that I had ever experienced before. His tongue against my clitoris hit every single nerve ending, creating a tingling release. My legs straightened and I held my breath for a moment in silence. I tightened my grip around his head with my legs and all the build-up I had felt inside finally released. My legs shook, and my mind went into a state of euphoria as I collapsed beneath him.

I smiled to myself with a final groan of satisfaction as I brought my legs back together, holding onto the euphoric feeling that would remain with me for the next few seconds, but the memory for a lifetime.

Casey exhaled with triumph and brought himself up face to face with me. He brushed the hair from my face and kissed me softly on my lips. I could taste a part of me on him. My eyes met his and we didn't break the contact. Without looking away, he filtered his fingers through mine, holding them above my head.

I let out an expressive groan as I felt him push his way inside.

"Oh my god, April." He kissed me harder, as he held himself deep inside for a few seconds.

That's so deep...

I tensed my whole body with a feeling that I had never experienced before. I could feel him pushing up against my cervix, but it didn't hurt. It was a pleasurable pain that I didn't want to end. I didn't want this night or us to end. I rolled my eyes back again. I brought myself back to the moment, fixating my eyes on him, as he did not take his gaze away from me. Have you ever been able to look into someone's eyes and weep because you can feel the love between two people? I felt it in that exact moment. We weren't fucking. This was love.

Don't admit it, April. It's too early to say anything...

Nothing beats the transparency between two people after having sex. You have opened up to each other physically and you both lie there for a moment whilst stuck in a heavenly sense of freedom. I was laid down with his arm wrapped around my body and my leg over his. I gently caressed his chest hair without any words being spoken. Everything was silent and perfect for a moment. That was until a German Shepherd managed to find us in our must vulnerable state.

"Shit!" I panicked.

I grabbed hold of my dress, throwing it back over my head as quick as I could, as Casey was still coming to grasp with what was happening. He likewise pulled up his boxers, tripping over his own feet and landing on the ground again.

"Alfie! Over here, boy!" I heard the owner call the German Shepherd back. It was clear that the owner saw and knew exactly what was happening, but thankfully, he chose to ignore it and move on to save us from sheer embarrassment.

Casey laughed as he continued getting himself dressed again.

"I guess we should probably make a move," he decided.

I nodded in agreement, with my cheeks blushed red, wanting to swiftly remove those few seconds from my brain, but how could I?

I saw another side to Casey on the drive home that night. A side which showed his compassion, understanding and wanting to learn more about me. He wanted clarification on what I enjoyed and what I didn't enjoy so much. I was honest with him throughout the whole thing. I explained that even though I was shy and inexperienced, especially when it comes to fancy restaurants, I still appreciated him trying to bring me out of my shell. It meant that I would learn more about the things I can do and the food and drinks that I could enjoy. As for the sex, he didn't need to ask, but he did. He wanted to make sure I was happy and comfortable and, for the first time ever, I felt like I could be open with him about anything. In other relationships, sex is just sex. It happens and then it is never talked about, but how are both partners meant to know what their spouse does and doesn't enjoy if they never discuss it after? I didn't realise that myself until now.

He pulled up outside my house and I stalled leaving the car. I didn't want to say goodbye, but I knew I couldn't be too needy in that moment. I needed this time to think about today and plan for the next time before letting him stay over. Without needing to say it, I knew that Casey felt that way, too.

I lay in my bed that night, tossing and turning without sleep. This time, it wasn't a stressful, restless sleep. Instead, I was restless with giddiness. It had been a while since I last felt this way and I never wanted this feeling to leave. I know that this feeling would eventually fade with time, but I didn't want it *all* to leave. I hoped and prayed that if this was meant to be, that I would still hold on to this "honeymoon" emotion about him.

It was late, but I unlocked my phone, opening the text messages to Bernadette. All I knew was that I needed to speak to someone about how I felt. I wanted to brag.

April: It was amazing!!!

Sent. Now go to sleep, April.

Parents' love

Casey: Good morning, beautiful. Thank you for the best night of my life, so far.

What an amazing text to wake up to, but the thought of things moving far too quickly was quite fearful. Either way, my heart got the better of my mind as I bit my bottom lip, pulling my phone close to my chest, thinking about last night all over again.

April: And thank you! Any chance of seeing you today?

Casey: I can't sorry. I'm working today.

April: Working on a Saturday? What do you do exactly?

Casey: Joiner. I'm just in the process of working on a unique staircase for a client. I will call you later though, red.

See, April... It's too soon to be pushing things forward. You've only just found out what he does for a living.

I decided not to waste my day, replaying yesterday's antics in my head over and over. Instead, I decided to drive myself to Bernadette's to replay yesterday's antics to her, so we could both foolishly enjoy the moments together.

Bernadette sat in her living room clutching at her cushion, listening to my story intently. After explaining, she sat there with a million and one questions, half of which I didn't know the answer to myself.

"Are you two a thing or a fling?" she dubiously asked.

I shrugged my shoulders in response, but I couldn't hold back the smile between the uncertainty.

"You dirty devil!" she stated, throwing the cushion at me. I didn't believe I would find someone who was more excited about me having sex, other than me.

"We're not a thing, Bernie," I interrupted.

Her smile faded, not understanding why.

"I want it to be, but it's too early to jump into another relationship. We need to see how things go." I needed Bernadette to understand everything that was running through my head. Partially because I wanted her to understand my reasoning, but also because I wanted her to be that confirming secondary voice to say, "just do it". Instead, she agreed with me and verified that it was too early.

"Have you told any of the girls or your parents?" she asked tentatively.

"Other girls? I rarely speak to Hannah or Niamh anymore. Not since I split up with Matthew and I was thinking about calling on my parents after here, but I don't think I will mention Casey just yet. They will probably judge him before meeting him, as they usually do. I have probably done something that they are disappointed in too."

The conversation had soon diminished from being ecstatic to being very serious very quickly. In saying this, I could always rely on Bernie to be there as support for me, no matter what. I knew that she mainly sat and listened to what I needed to say, but sometimes that's all we need… a listener.

On my way home, I did call on my parents. I do love them and not just because they are my parents. I grew up in a strict but fair home that taught me everything I needed as an adult to mature and become an independent woman. However, I have got to admit that I have built a much better relationship with them by not living with them. Part of this is due to the fact that when I can feel an argument about to begin, I can grab my car keys and make a dart for the door.

I pulled my car into the main yard in front of the farmer's house. After switching off the ignition, I could already hear my parents' TV turned all the way up. Without knocking, I walked inside to find my mum in her armchair and on the other side, my father was sitting in his armchair entranced by his favourite show on the screen, Steptoe & Son. I dropped my keys and phone on the side table next to my dad to see if he would even flinch at my appearance, but again, there was nothing.

My mother greeted me with a hug and switched on the kettle for a cup of tea, whilst my dad was still none the wiser that I was even in the house. Everything could be resolved with a cup of tea in this house. Are you upset? Have a cup of tea. Have you got amazing news? Have a cup of tea. It even went as far as are you too warm? Have a cup of tea, it cools you down. I swear my parents had a cup of tea excuse for everything. Regardless, it was times like this that I enjoyed. I sat down with my mum at the table in the kitchen with a cup of tea warming between the palms of my hands.

Once the episode had finished, my father made his way from the living room into the kitchen. He tapped me on the shoulder, greeting me with "Hello, Goldie!" It was an old nickname my dad gave me that had always stuck. Little Goldilocks and the three bears. I was always told how I would cry and cry until I had everything just right when I was younger. This included my bath being too hot or too cold, my food being too hot or too cold. The list could honestly go on and even now I'm almost thirty, I was still greeted with my old nickname.

Some time had passed by as my bottom started becoming numb from sitting on the same wooden chair for too long. My parents seemed happy to see me and I didn't want to leave just yet. Not when I can share good times with them like this.

"Your father came across an old photo album from when you were just a nipper. Do you want to look?" my mother asked.

"Oh dear! Let's see them then," I chuckled.

My mum lifted herself from the table, and made her way over to the living room storage cabinet to flick through the photo albums until she found the right one. I sat waiting patiently with my dad at the table as my mum stumbled around.

"Hello?"

"Hello?" I responded to my mum, as I wondered who she was speaking to.

"Oh sorry, I must have picked up April's phone by accident. I'm her mother."

Oh no! That will be Casey off work.

I tried to remain calm, but I could feel the heat from the cup between my hands rush through my whole body. My face was on fire and the colour interconnected with the feeling. I removed my hands from the cup, placing them between my legs to try to control my twitchy foot bouncing on the floor. I couldn't look at my dad, as I knew he would already have so many questions. He already knows that I only spend time with Bernadette now, since I tried to focus back on myself.

My mother handed my phone over to me with an awaited look on her face.

"Hi Casey, I'm sorry. I can't talk now. I'm just with my parents. I will speak to you later." Before even allowing him time to speak to me, I cut the call. I could see my parents leaning further in across the table to listen to him, and the last thing I needed right now was petrol to ignite the fire that was about to happen.

It was silent for a moment, as I fought to think of any conversation to distract them from the obvious. It was too late; my mother had already begun.

"So… Who is Casey?"

My mind went blank. I couldn't think. What was the right thing to say to my parents without an argument starting?

"I should hope it isn't another love-sick man you're jumping in bed with!" my dad obscenely jumped in.

"No! He's just..."

What do I say?

This is not the way I wanted to introduce Casey to my parents. I quickly pre-emptively sorted ideas in my head to weigh up the negative and positive outcomes of what could be mentioned. Why should I have to be afraid to open up to my parents?

"Okay, he's not just some man." I watched as my parents' faces turned to a look of disappointment already, without giving me chance to continue speaking.

"I met him not long ago, at Bernadette's party."

"You didn't cheat on Matthew, did you?" my dad crudely questioned, without giving a moment to listen to me.

"Of course not!" I bellowed.

I took a breath before trying to explain more calmly. "We have been talking a little bit and we went on our first date yesterday. It's nothing serious, but there's potential. I wasn't going to mention anything just yet because I wanted the opportunity to learn more about him myself and see how things work out before making any commitments." I knew I was becoming short-tempered. I shot my parents a warning look, but I knew that it wouldn't mean anything to them.

"So, you're bed hopping until you find the right man, then?" my dad started the argument.

Leave April, before harmful words are said.

"I knew you wouldn't listen! I think it's my time to leave…" I waited for a response, but there was nothing. I grabbed my phone and keys and left for the door.

Like I said before, I love my parents, but I love them better when I live away from their home. Unfortunately, I didn't have the same relationship with my parents as most others would have. I have never been able to fully open up to them about anything that happens in my life. I tried to hold back the tears on the drive home. I wasn't sure if it was my hormones, or the fact my life has been a rollercoaster ride these last few months. I suppose what hurt most of all was getting up to leave and having no encouragement from my parents to stay so they could understand me. Majority of my life had been spent trying to please my parents, but I came to a point of realisation that I would never be able to fulfil this.

I collapsed onto my bed, with my eyes blurred and bloodshot red with tears of anger. I crawled onto my side, holding myself like a foetus until my surroundings darkened into a peaceful sleep.

Sleeping is a lot like death. It is a moment of rest and peace, when all the pain and torment has finally left. It was cold. I couldn't feel any air around my skin, only a dense, thick substance surrounding me. I couldn't escape, so I stopped fighting. How could I breathe when there was no air surrounding me? Was something trying to keep me alive? My speech and movement were restricted, as I allowed the ground to swallow me and finish me, as it saw fit.

As I let my body weight give way beneath me, a muscle-like movement kept pulling around me, as though it was trying to force me further down into the depths. I could move my toes! I wriggled around as I felt myself slowly being freed, but I still couldn't look down to see where or how. I began falling and as I left the black hole, I took a deep intake of air again, breathing it into my lungs. I couldn't scream and I also didn't feel any pain, as my body hit against the ground with force. My dress was no longer white but brown, covered in the Earth's soil.

I gazed around warily at my surroundings. I'm in the forest again, except it's darker than before. I could see no grass along the ground, only dandelions. The yellow daylight nature had transitioned to white dispersed seeds, which, when still on the flower, mirrored the moonlight. However, when the wind blew the seed from the flower, they floated around in formation like fairies at night. It brought back my childhood years, whereby I would collect the seeds on a cloudy day as they floated above me, and I contained them in a lunch box. As a child, my imaginative mind saw them as wishful fairies. I would make a wish and release some into the air from my lunchbox and hope that my wish would come true. Now, as I lie here in the cold dirt, I could only wish for familiarity. Something to warm my emotions. I lay my head down onto the ground, giving in, as I felt the dandelion's seeds blow against my hair and disappear into the night sky.

Warm air brushed against my ear. Opening my eyes, I came face to face with the stag again. Its eyes were filled with worry as they focused in with mine. I raised my hand to make contact with its nose, but it jolted back in fear. Watching my every move, the stag slowly rejoined me by my side. It steadied its head closer to mine, as I reached further out to provide comfort.

Bang

Gunshot! My eyes did not move from the stag's glare. Its dilated pupils became constricted within seconds, as its natural instinct to run again came to focus. The stag disappeared again into the dark woods.

Bang

I was alone and now in fear of what was around. My heart raced as I nervously twisted my head in all angles to see. The banging continued as my mind came to consciousness from a dream-like state.

The door!

I jumped out of bed to run to my front door. I opened it to see Casey stood in worry.

I forgot to call him back!

I could see that he had been short of breath with worry and his eyes looked full of distress. I tucked myself into one side to allow him entrance into my home. Casey held his hands on my arms, restricting them to the sides of my body. He took a good look at my face and wandered through my eyes, into the uncertainty. He pulled me into his chest, stroking through my knotted hair with one hand.

"I'm so sorry, April!"

I narrowed my eyes into his chest, as I began pulling away from his grip.

"Why are you sorry?" I asked.

"I didn't realise you were at your parents. I understand it's still too early to bring me into your life and your family's life. I feel like I annoyed you after the phone call and then not hearing from you…"

"No, no!" I interrupted him to spare the worry. "I mean yes, I was hoping to break the news to my parents later down the line, but I'm not annoyed with you in the slightest. I'm sorry I was short with you and didn't call back."

Our elevated emotional distress began to quieten after sitting down to talk, with a cup of tea, of course. I found it strange, yet enlightening, to have an interest in someone who also has an interest in my life and communicates it to me. Are my emotions getting the better of my mind? I suppose only time will tell.

A blanket of darkness covered the skies, and I heard my boiler kick in to warm the house. I looked over at Casey, who clearly became more comfortable with his surroundings, making himself at home. I stood up as I glimpsed Casey watching my every move from behind.

I leaned over the sofa, curving my body as I did. Grabbing hold of a fleece blanket, I returned to Casey's side, wrapping the blanket around him.

"Do you need to leave?" I earnestly asked.

Casey shook his head from side to side. "Not if you don't want me to," he conscientiously added.

I leaned my head in closer, with my lips parted, hoping for reciprocation. I wasn't let down, as he brought the blanket over the both of us, dropping from the sofa onto the living room rug beneath us.

"Now I understand your name, April," he seductively said while grasping hold of me with his arms.

Surprised, yet very much intrigued, I cocked my head to one side, looking up at him for some kind of unravelment.

"Because just like the Spring, you are my new and brighter beginning."

I blushed at his interpretation of my name.

Calm the flutters, April.

I couldn't. I can't! I jumped up, kissing him harder with a more meaningful message behind my deep emotions. He slowed me down with the movement of his lips against mine. The pace became much more intimate with his arm around my back and the other undoing the buttons of my shirt. I closed my eyes, knowing he was looking at me in a new light. I didn't want to see the thoughts on his face. I inhaled, pushing my breasts out more for his wanting touch. He grabbed hold of my right breast in his hand, caressing my areola until the nipple became erect for him. His head leaned in, licking the surrounding area. I pulled his head in further, with my hands gripping hold of his hair. I pulled the air in through my teeth, trying hard to control my pulsating body.

Carefully lowering me down onto my back again, he began unbuttoning my jeans. He thought I couldn't see his sly grin looking down at me as he finally removed the last of my clothing. A gentle, rhythmic motion with his tongue enticed me to sway my hips in accordance with his kisses.

This is what it means to be treated right, April. The man should put your needs before his own…

After laying there in wet pleasure, Casey cupped his arm under the arch of my back, picking me up and moving us both over to the large love seat that sat in the corner of my room. Looking at me intently in an upright position, he pushed his way inside of me and, to my astonishment, I could feel so much more inside. He brought my legs up so that they were bent, continuing in a slow motion inside of me.

His eyes fixated on mine, staring into the blue oceanic depths for answers. I searched through his eyes into the earth's core, trying to search for fate and thank him.

Why am I crying?

Have you ever been so happy and appreciative of a moment enough to cry? I have, but never during sex. I felt more than just satisfaction from this man, and I struggled to slow down my emotions.

He released from me, exhaling in triumph. I rolled myself into the grasp of his arms, inhaling his scent into my lungs. Nuzzling my face against his chest, I managed to drift off into a peaceful sleep.

I woke the following morning, finding myself cocooned in my fluffy blanket, alone. I moved my tongue around inside my mouth, to see if I had bad morning breath. Squinting my eyes, I tried to observe my surroundings.

Where is he?

I came to a stand, still naked from the night before. My legs trembled as I ambled to the kitchen where I opened the door to smell…

Mmmm… Scrambled eggs!

Casey jolted back as he saw me in his peripheral vision.

"I know, I look like Fiona turning back into an ogre in the morning," I joked.

Casey laughed, looking back at me again properly.

"Quite the opposite, red," he reassured me.

I watched over his shoulder, judging his every move, wanting to learn more about his routines. All I wanted was to drag this morning out so that he wouldn't need to leave. I peered over at the other side of my worktop to find my first aid box had been pulled out of the cupboard and opened up. I couldn't see that Casey had injured himself and he seemed OK.

Baffled, I had to ask.

"Are you hurt?" I asked, whilst pointing over at the box.

Casey looked at me apologetically for going through my cupboards.

"Sorry, red. I found some Deep Heat cream in there and I just needed some for my knees. All the custom work I've taken on recently has got the better of me."

Workaholic perhaps? Should this be a potential red flag? Is he work first, lady second? I suppose as a positive, I could see this as he doesn't have time to look for other women if he is keeping himself focused. Something was determined to tell me there's something more behind this silhouette of a man. Details hadn't yet come into play.

Think positively, April. He's a good guy.

"My friend is having a stopover Halloween party, if you would like to join me as a plus one?" He quickly and successfully changed the subject that only moments ago was bouncing around in the room.

I agreed to his invite without hesitation before my mind faded into overthinking mode.

Well done, April! You probably look desperate now. I've let this man step into my life too quickly. Whatever happened to focusing on myself? But it is so hard when he's so good at focusing on me...

I shook my head, trying to get rid of the voices in my head, arguing on my conscience. It didn't take long though before I let my mind drift off again into an imaginary state. This time, thinking about what to wear for a Halloween party. It felt like a lifetime ago that I went to a Halloween party. I wasn't even sure I had anything to wear. Even after Casey left that afternoon to return home, I repeatedly kept thinking about a costume and different scenarios that could play out at the Halloween party. I have never heard Casey talk about his parents, but this opportunity to see his friends for the first time was just as nerve-wracking.

I found myself pacing in circles, biting at my fingernails, just thinking about it. I completely switched myself off from the outside world, as mini-April's ran riot in my head with counter arguments.

Isn't it funny that when you're alone, a new you will become present that nobody has seen before? You think about things that would never come to mind in the presence of someone else, because you become influenced by conversation in a natural flow. On your own, all your personal thoughts come into play, drowning you, especially at night.

A new you

Its sharpened, acute edge became more pronounced as I allowed it to emerge from its protective case. As it emerged, it was already full of the Scarlet red colour, that would have represented the blood of Christ. I held it up to my face, as I slowly and precisely applied pressure. I couldn't make any mistakes, not now. I needed to steady my hand. The blood red stained my lips, completing my Halloween outfit. A beautiful witch.

I took another glimpse of myself in the mirror, feeling proud of my makeup. I posed ridiculously at myself to see how I would look to others if I smiled, frowned, pouted. Is that just me or do other people do that too?

I checked my phone for the time and readily set my location on Uber to be able to get a lift to Casey's friend's house. We agreed to meet there, since he needed to help his friend set up the party. It also gave me the opportunity to pre-drink and steady my nerves. The taxi pulled up outside the front of my house.

Right on schedule!

It is true what they say: You can judge a person in seven seconds. I always say hello in a very cheerful voice to a taxi driver and dependent on their response, it tells me exactly how the rest of the drive will be. Unfortunately, I had the silent type this time, but it allowed me time in my own thoughts to prepare for an introduction with Casey's friends. (Not that I had been doing that all day anyway). The roads became dark in an area that I did not recognise. I scanned the area for any indication that I was heading the right way. Reassurance prevailed as colourful, mesmerising lights illuminated the road ahead.

At least it's easy enough for you to know which house, April.

There were already so many people at the party and those that had already set up camp in the large garden. I filtered through all the people outside, awkwardly trying to find someone I knew. My head span from left to right more times than a barn owl. That was until my heart jumped at the feeling of a hand come across my shoulder. I spun around to see Bernie behind me.

"You made it!" she rejoiced. She jumped in for a hug and I could already smell alcohol on her breath.

"Guess who I found here," she impatiently asked, wanting a response immediately.

Before I had a chance to answer, she pointed her finger in the direction of a man facing his back to us. It wasn't Casey but somehow, he looked familiar. The mysterious man turned around, allowing me to quickly observe his facial features. My jaw dropped in realisation, but Bernadette excitedly jumped with joy beside me.

"Henry! Come over here!" she demanded.

Henry's hazel eyes looked up in my direction and I saw a smile grow on his face, as I was still trying to control my own facial expressions. I watched as he pushed through everyone around him, apprehensively approaching me for what seemed to be an inviting hug.

I simultaneously widened my arms to allow for a reunion hug.

"April!" he yelled down my ear, deafening me. He had clearly already had a few beers, given that his self-control for voice volume had disappeared.

Still in shock, I was trying to remember how long it had been since I had last seen Henry. We studied together in college when we both took an interest in music, so it had at least been a decade. Not a lot changed about him, apart from growing a very messy and frizzy dark beard. His hair was still a wavy, dirty blonde, but his smile was still the same… Contagious.

After discovering how we had both come to be at this party, Bernadette agreed to get drinks for us all. In the meantime, I kept looking around for Casey. I couldn't see him anywhere in sight. I would have text him but considering how long it had been since seeing Henry, I thought it would be rude to start texting. I could see how eager Henry was in trying to catch me up with the last ten years of his life. It was interesting to hear how he had taken a seriousness in his music after college, unlike me. He went on to practice guitar and perform his own songs. He had also dropped on with opportunities to perform at some local gigs. I only wish he had his guitar with him now, so I could experience the story in the flesh. He did disappointingly admit that to make enough income, he was also working 40 hours a week at a little shop in town, but needs must.

"I need a wee!" I announced, after finishing off the last bit of whisky and coke that Bernie had poured for me.

Standing up, I made my way over to the house, meandering my way through the rooms to find the bathroom. After finally finding it, I was halted by the shouting of someone on the other side of the door, telling me it's already in use. I slumped my weight back against the wall, waiting for them to come out of the bathroom.

"Enjoying the party?" I heard someone approach me.

I looked down the landing to see Casey stood at the stairs with a stern look about him.

"There you are!" I merrily celebrated at seeing him at last.

I didn't receive the same excited tone from Casey as he came to my side. "I've just been downstairs with the lads," he explained. "Who were you with outside?"

I didn't understand why, but I felt a sense of guilt inside, even though I had nothing to be guilty of. This was perhaps a resultant traumatic response I have from my previous relationship. I had nothing to hide from Casey and I was happy to be honest with him.

"Henry. I went to college with him. Bernie found him here and introduced us both again!" I shouldn't need to justify myself, but his look of concern was spiked with jealousy.

There was no response from Casey. I hesitated to look up at him, worried that his face would be full of anger, making me feel upset and guilty for something I shouldn't feel guilty about.

Instead, I was taken back by his genuine smile, as he looked me up and down.

"You look absolutely stunning, Miss Jones. I can't wait to introduce you to my friends…"

I exhaled after holding my breath with concerned hesitation.

Casey is not your ex. He will not guilt trip you…

Casey waited as I finished in the bathroom and checked my makeup in the mirror. He held out his hand to me, in a silent announcement that he was proud for us to be seen. We walked through the house into the garden. Bemused, I looked around to see everyone's stares as they saw us both holding hands. I held Casey's hand a little tighter as I brought him forward in front of me, to introduce him to Henry first. Bernie stood there and handed me another cup of whisky and coke with her jaw dropped, holding in an internal happy scream that we were holding hands.

"Henry, this is Casey." I stopped there, not knowing how to end that sentence. Can I even say boyfriend yet?

Henry held out his hand to Casey, shaking firmly while keeping his eyes fixed on mine.

"So, this is what you've been getting up to the last ten years is it then, April?" he asked.

"Not so much ten years, maybe the last few weeks," I corrected him. A tweak of embarrassment flooded my body as I heard myself say that out loud... *Only the last few weeks.*

Casey did not spend much time with Henry before asking me to meet his friends. I gave Henry a goodbye hug, unsure whether I would see him again that night.

Casey's friends took a much different approach to introducing themselves to me. These were what we would refer to as "the lads". Zeeky (short for Geeky Zekariah), Vanny Danny (nickname due to his obsessions with Vee-Dub vans) and finally Big Billy (I don't think I need to *expand* on this one). Each one of them stood there with egos bigger than Billy himself. Zeeky and Danny were the type to spend each night at the gym flirting with anything and everything, thinking they could own it all. Physically, they were all of a similar age, in their 30s, yet their maturity was at a much lower comparison. Casey didn't seem to be anything like them, but perhaps I hadn't seen that side yet.

As much as I didn't appreciate "the lads" personalities, it didn't mean that I couldn't get along with them. They were funny and comfortable to be around, but reliable and loyal? 100% not. My night was not a disappointment, though. I continued to drink past my limit. The line in which you know to slow down, but not tonight. Casey didn't fail to reciprocate this, continuing to hold me close through the night, twirling me around in his grasp to the rhythm of the music.

Bernie would come and join me occasionally for a dance before disappearing again into the night. She had always been able to mix well with other people. I found it more difficult, but with more alcohol in my system, it became considerably easier.

After prolonged dancing, I fell into Casey's arms in exhaustion.

"I need a drink," I gasped for air.

Casey smirked, looking down at me before proceeding to give me a kiss on the forehead.

"As if you haven't had enough already," he mocked.

Scrunching up my face to him, I released from his grip to try to prove a point. In doing so, I stumbled over to the table, pouring myself another drink. I couldn't steady or control my pour, so I ended up with 50% gin and 50% tonic.

Oh well, it's like water now!

Before chugging my drink back in regret, I was tapped on the shoulder. I turned to see Henry. I tried to focus all my senses as though I was a drunk driver being pulled over. No matter how hard I tried, I struggled to understand him.

"Huh?" I abruptly interrupted him.

"I said do you remember us dancing to this music in the recording studio in our media sessions?"

I threw my arm onto Henry's chest whilst uncontrollably laughing.

"Those were the days," I spluttered the drink back into my cup of death.

I felt another hand reach around my waist, following around my body to face me. I looked up, regaining focus on Casey. He stood there with a stern look about him, but a sexy stern. Even though my vision was blurred, I was glad it was doubled so I could see this man twice. Casey removed my cup from my hand, placing it back onto the table, before I could force any more into my system.

"I think you've had enough now, babe."

My heart rushed at being called babe. This was the first time, and my drunken reaction was to look past Casey and at Henry, straightening my smile to avoid laughing.

"Babe... Did you hear that, Henry?" I burst out laughing.

I watched as Casey shook Henry's hand and wished him a good night. His next mission was to locate Bernie in all the crowd. She could have been anywhere at this point, but Casey managed to find her.

"I'm going to take April back to mine, Bernie. Anymore and she'll be throwing up."

I steadied myself, attempting to look as sober as possible. The harder I tried, the more I wobbled. Bernadette snorted out loud, knowing that Casey was right. Of course he was. He's Mr. Holmes, remember?

Bernie wrapped her arms around me tightly. It was her subtle way of telling me to be careful.

In the time it took for Casey to wish everyone farewell, book a taxi and the journey home, I managed to sober up somewhat and I was grateful that I had. I rested my head on Casey's shoulder on the way home, trying desperately not to fall asleep. I felt so comforted with his arm wrapped around my waist, holding me to his side firmly. He was warm and I felt safe by his side.

Focus, April! If you fall asleep now, you won't wake again until late into the morning.

Once we arrived at Casey's, he continued to assist me to the door, whilst messing around in his pocket for the house key. The door slowly opened as I stumbled in over the door frame. Casey continued to laugh at me, but I didn't even feel embarrassed at this point. Collapsing onto his sofa, I was hoping he would follow close behind to lie by my side. Instead, he made his way into the kitchen and turned on the oven. My eyes began drifting into a sleep until my sense of smell heightened.

"Are you putting chips on?" I asked curiously, but also greedily hoped I was correct.

"We've both drank more than double our body weight, red. We're probably best having something solid before a good night's sleep."

"I could think of something solid to eat," I chuckled with my eyes still closed.

There wasn't an answer and the room fell silent. I slowly began opening one eye to check around to find a figure in front of me blocking the living room light.

"Is that a promise?" Casey jokingly asked whilst leaning over me. I nodded slowly, whilst biting down onto my bottom lip. Casey didn't acknowledge this, but his act of control turned me on more. I returned to closing my eyes whilst smiling to myself at the possibilities. If he wasn't prepared to give me anything now, he could at least leave me with my imagination.

Chips always taste the best after a few drinks. I dunked my chips into a side dip of ketchup on the plate and ate as though I was in a race with an older sibling. After having food, I felt more awake to be able to engage in conversation with Casey and appreciate this moment with him. We quickly finished the food before returning to the kitchen to wash. Nobody likes to wake up to dirty dishes.

I stood over the sink, my hands fully submersed in soapy water. I felt his arms reaching around me from behind. Leaving the plate in the sink, I raised my arms above my head. Turning my neck gently, I felt the warmth of his breath against my cheek.

"Did I ever tell you I love a woman in black?" he playfully whispered in my ear.

"Have I ever told you that you constantly give me butterflies?" I playfully answered.

I'll regret that one in the morning!

"I want to show you something," he sincerely requested. Grabbing hold of my hand, he led me up the stairs with no lights on to guide the way. I carefully followed in his footsteps, my mind fluttering with too many ideas at once.

Then he switched on the bedroom light…

The red and white bedding was freshly made, and everything was tucked in neatly without creases. However, what caught my eyes more was what was scattered on the bed… Real and beautiful red rose petals.

Was he expecting me to come back here tonight?

I couldn't care less. My eyes felt heavy with tears as I tried to hold back on my emotions. I couldn't. This was the first time I had ever been treated like this and, for the first time ever, I felt valued. I held my hand up to my mouth in utter disbelief, as I buried my head into his chest to hide the tears in my eyes. Casey lifted my chin with his thumb and wiped my tears away with his sleeve.

"I'm glad you came back with me tonight, otherwise this would have been a very self-romantic night for me," he humorously added.

I giggled whilst still trying to find the right words to explain to him how much this had meant to me, but I didn't need to. He knew.

"No-nobody's ever done anything like this for me." My bottom lip quivered, and my voice trembled as I let myself fall into his arms.

"Let me show you how much you mean to me."

Brushing my hair behind my ear, he lifted me onto the bed, climbing above me. He kissed my lips, sweet, wet, soft kisses. The sort of kisses that made you feel as though a cupid had struck you with a love poison tipped arrow straight into the heart. The poison began making its way down through my body, just as his kisses followed.

I held his hair in my hands, grabbing softly, looking down at him giving me all the attention and pleasure that I never even asked for. Sweet, wet, soft kisses…

I tensed my body before physically showing him evidence of my satisfaction. I lay in euphoria as my eyes closed and the smile on my face would not disappear. I removed my hands from his hair, bringing them up above my head in release.

Casey lay by my side, stroking my face slowly and in silence. I released a whispered groan of enjoyment.

"That Henry definitely has a thing for you." He broke the silence.

Couldn't words wait in this beautiful moment?

"No, he doesn't! We haven't seen each other for years and we had so much to catch up on," I abruptly stated, whilst defending Henry.

"I realise that, but his eyes said something different, red."

Mr Holmes is looking through people again.

"Is somebody a little jealous?" I teased him, curious to know the answer.

"Maybe a little, but then again, I'm the one that has you in bed, not him."

That was true, but his boasting almost came across like he thought he owned me.

"Are you falling for me, Mr Woods?"

"What if I said, yes?"

Here we go, using the Socratic method – answering a question, by asking another question. Ultimately, to make the interviewer the interviewee… Clever boy.

"Well then, I suppose we are best discussing our futures and our individual goals. If I take the next step, I want it to be the right step, Mr Woods."

For the next few hours, I never managed to close my eyes to sleep, but I didn't want to. I wanted to have this deep conversation. I wanted to know about his thoughts on marriage, children, responsibilities, interests, his weaknesses… Everything.

It may seem silly that I wanted to know all these things, but after one failed long-term relationship and almost being 30 years old, I didn't want another mistake. I didn't want to be two years down the line to realise we both want to live separate lifestyles. I needed to know, and Casey was more than happy to involve himself and learn more about me, too.

1. Affection – CHECK!
2. Sex – CHECK!
3. Communication – CHECK!
4. Empathy – I need to see more.
5. Notice – CHECK!
6. Trust – I need to see more.

4 out of 6, not too bad at all, Mr Woods.

I woke the following morning, remembering that this was my first night with Casey. A smile grew on my face as I turned my body to look at Casey, lying next to me. To my surprise, he was already awake and looking at me dreamily with those jade green eyes.

"Good morning, beautiful," he softly spoke.

He caressed the side of my body with his finger, following the curves up to my face.

"I might have to buy fake rose petals next time,"

Confused, I scrunched my face as I looked up at him. He smiled and his eyes directed us down towards the bed sheets. Blood red stained bed sheets covered us. We must have pressed and rubbed the colour out of the petals.

I wasn't sure whether to laugh or to take him seriously and help him to try to remove the stains. I started lifting myself out of bed to find some white vinegar, before I felt a pull bringing me back into his arms.

"Where are you going?" he asked.

"I was going to fetch some white vinegar or any other stain remover you have here to help get the stains out."

His eyes softened and his smirk grew across his face. "I like the stains… It makes it more memorable."

A warm feeling spread inside me at the thought of him wanting to keep hold of things that remind him of me.

Where has this man been all my life?

A father's approval

It had been two months into seeing Casey that we finally decided he should meet my parents. I still hadn't seen my parents since I last left their home with an unresolved argument. If my parents didn't agree with something, they chose to avoid the conversation as a means to let go and forget it had ever happened.

I wasn't sure how they would react to meeting Casey, but I thought it would be wiser to turn up unannounced at my parents' house. If I pre-warned my parents that I was bringing Casey, it gave them time to pre-meditate about what to say and how best to judge him, without first meeting him.

I had never seen Casey so flustered before, but the idea of him feeling nervous about meeting my parents made me certain that this was the right choice. He was physically showing me how much this first impression means to him and how desperately he wanted to try with my parents. He must have showered twice already because he had been sweating with anxiety. One thing I had learned about this man was that he copes with stress by using humour. I took this to both of our advantage when discussing difficult matters, by adding jokes to the equation. It had helped calm more than one situation.

"I've seen you push out a constipated shit with less stress on that face of yours." I looked over to hope for a smile and I wasn't disappointed to see a smirk beginning to break free on his face.

"I'm sorry, I'm usually better than this, but I don't want this to go wrong. I want a life with you, April."

"And I want a life with you, regardless of my parents' opinion," I tried to reassure him.

"But having their approval makes things easier," he mumbled to himself.

He was right but I knew deep down my parents would like him and I also knew that given time, they will also learn why I have come to "love" Casey the way I do. I felt as though I knew I loved Casey at that time, but we both agreed to not say it so early. I still have no idea why. If you know, you know, right?

Rather than using the term *love*, we both humorously used alternatives. It added a light feeling to the passion we had for each other. We would make remarks such as "I am infatuated by you" in a sense of tiptoeing around the commitment of "love". Looking back, it seemed silly, really. We knew how we both really felt, but we were both too scared to make a commitment so early on into the relationship. Even though everything else we said or did bellowed out the love we had for each other.

My dad was always right about that. He had always taught me from a young age that 'love is the most powerful word there is. That one word means a lifetime with one person, through the good times and the bad. It means a commitment to share, build, give up, learn and if you think you've already learnt it all, you are not ready for love. Love is a lifetime of learning about the person closest to you and learning their desires and their sacrifices for the relationship. It's a simple four-letter word, that has so much more meaning to its simplicity.'

On the drive to my parents, I kept reassuring Casey by holding his hand and rubbing his thumb with mine. I would bring his hand up to my mouth and kiss his knuckles softly. I ran out of words of encouragement, but I hoped my actions gave him the reassurance he needed.

I walked through the door first into my parent's house, as Casey followed closely behind.

"Hello, dear," my mother greeted me, before a shocked look flashed across her face, seeing Casey stood behind me.

My mother didn't worry me, it was my dad's thoughts on the situation that worried me more.

"I'm sorry, I don't think we've met. I'm Lorraine, April's mum." My mother held out her hand to Casey to greet him.

"Mum, where's dad?" I timidly asked. Without realising, I disturbed the first meeting and impression between both Casey and my mum.

"Around the back, sweetheart," my mum answered me without taking her eyes off Casey.

"It's very nice to meet you, Mrs Jones. I'm Casey." I looked back at him, as he pulled an uneasy smile to try to impress as best as he could. I held onto his hand, and I wasn't entirely sure if it was me that was shaking or Casey, as I led us all around to the back of the house to meet my dad.

My dad was sitting at the open leaf table with a newspaper in front of him, absorbing all the social gossip from recent local farce.

"Mike, this is Casey," my mother tentatively introduced.

I began feeling sweaty with nerves. God only knows how Casey must be feeling after taking two showers already. I stood close to Casey to provide support and reassurance. My father lowered the newspaper, making eye contact with Casey, before acknowledging my existence in the silent room. I wanted to say something, but what?

I watched as my father raised the papers up in front of his face, ignorantly, so as not to approach Casey in a friendly manner when talking to him.

"Hello daughter… And hello Casey," he added without another single word to help incur a meaningful conversation.

I watched as Casey hesitantly looked across at me, slowly shrugging his shoulders in uncertainty. I could see his struggle and I wanted to help, but I could not think of words to say. I kept my head down, whilst taking a step forward to cover for Casey.

"It's a pleasure to meet you both. What are you reading there, Mr Jones?"

Casey's unsteady voice echoed in the room as he attempted to make a connection.

I looked over at my mother, who stood there anticipating my father's input as anxiously as me.

"A load of shit! That's all I can say. Why don't you take a seat, Casey?"

My father folded the papers over, throwing them into the centre of the table, engaging with the people in the room. That's all it took. "What are you reading there?" is all that needed to be said to show my dad he wanted to try to make this work. The longer we sat at the table, the more relaxed we began feeling. I managed to feel comfortable in introducing Casey, finally.

My mum didn't say a great deal, but I could tell by her face and interest with the conversation that she was happy for me.

When the conversation had finally fallen to a comfortable silence, my father looked up at me with concern in his narrowed eyes. He paused for a moment to think before speaking.

"April, my love?"

"Yes, dad?" I acknowledged the concern in his tone.

"Are you happy? Are you *truly* happy?"

A smile broke out over my face, knowing that he was lovingly asking, as he had my feelings close to his heart.

"I'm at my happiest that I could be, dad." I held my hands out, with a soft look, asking for my dad to hold my hands in promise and acceptance. He reciprocated by holding onto my hands and squeezing them tight. He smiled back and I watched his eyes soften from the narrowed frown that was showing only a few moments ago. Although it didn't take long for that look of happiness to disappear, as he turned to Casey with a look of warning…

"And your intentions, Casey?"

I gulped and my hands started to become clammy in the clench of my dad's grasp. I couldn't release myself to look at Casey, as my dad had hold of me, as though he didn't want to let me go in fear of losing his only daughter.

"You see that smile that you shared with your daughter? I want to keep that smile glowing on her face forever more…"

I'm speechless…

In that moment, not only did I know it was right, but my parents also accepted Casey with open arms, in the knowledge that Casey was not to break that promise to my dad.

I lay alongside Casey that night, sharing a moment of warmth and fulfillment between us. As I looked into his jade green eyes, it became easier to see the truth through the forest trees. Everything became more visible to the naked eye. I felt entranced by him, and I prayed that I wasn't being hypnotized by a fake love.

I closed my eyes, breathing in his scent of cedarwood shower gel. Being enclosed in his hold made me feel too warm, but I didn't want to break away. I wanted to feel this positive energy and absorb the smell.

I felt a passing wind, brushing the smell of cedarwood against me. I opened my eyes to find myself on my hands and knees between cedar trees. The sun was setting, and the darkness started closing in on me. I tried to stand and run, but I didn't know how and even though I felt a fear of something, I couldn't understand what it was that I needed to run away from.

I became paralysed in my own body, as it hurt to crawl across the ground to escape from an unknown fear that was following me. Every time I tried to scream, only a whisper would come out of my mouth.

Bang

The sound echoed through my body, as though I had been shot at myself. I could feel the pain passing through me, making any sudden movements unbearable. I lay still on the ground, listening for any sounds closing in on me.

crunch

That was from in front… I didn't have the courage to lift my head to look. If I can't see them, they can't see me. It's strange that even as an adult, we may refer back to our childhood thought processes, even when we know it isn't true.

I slowly lifted my head to face my fear. To my gratitude, I came to find the stag stood in front of me. This time it wasn't looking at me, but its piercing eyes had widened, staring past me in an intense silence. The stag itself was frozen and its eyes would not blink, in fear that if it takes one look away, this could be the end.

I lay in distress, knowing that even if I could stand to move, I shouldn't. The longer I tried to hold my breath, the harder it became. A small whimper escaped my mouth. The stag stopped staring and turned its head in my direction in a small gesture as if to say, "please don't."

Bang

"April, are you OK?"

I jolted upright in bed, gasping for air. Casey wrapped his arm around me until he realised that my body was wet from sweat. I looked back at the fitted sheet to see a sweat patch from where I had been lying in his arms.

"Bad dream," I exhaled.

My body was in shock as I tried to calm myself from an unconscious fear.

"I'll get you a glass of water." He helpfully jumped from bed to ensure I had everything I needed.

I began lying back in our bed against the cold patch that was beneath me. I closed my eyes whilst taking deep breaths to bring myself back to a normal state.

Bang

My eyes opened wider than before. Was that noise real? Was I dreaming again? I stayed still for a moment trying to work out my surroundings.

"Shit!" I heard Casey bellow from downstairs.

I leaped out of bed in a state of confusion trying to understand what was happening. As I stood at the top of the stairs, I saw a figure lying down in a fetal position in the darkness.

"Casey?" I whimpered.

I switched on the light and ran downstairs. He was holding on to his leg as the source of pain. His knee looked inflamed, and I could see him trying to brush past the pain, gritting his teeth. I held my hand over his knee and looked at Casey, waiting for an answer.

"Bloody knees!" he angrily ejected.

"Casey, that looks sore. Did you fall?"

He stayed quiet for a moment, as though he was hesitant to talk to me.

"My knee has been sore from work, but I must have slipped, and I've made it worse now."

I was unsure how to help provide a resolution if it was work-related. I knew he loved his work, but I also knew it was taking a toll on his physical body. I grabbed some frozen veg from the freezer and placed it over his knee.

Kissing him softly on the cheek, I asked him to go to the doctors. This wasn't the first time I asked, but his stubbornness prevailed once more as he refused. All I would hear from him is "what's the point if I'm going back to work and it'll cause pain again eventually, anyway."

Sometimes persistence is key, as I asked him again if he would see a doctor for me. Even if the doctor could provide a recommendation for the best gel treatment or pain killers, it would help him to control the pain he is suffering from.

"I'll go tomorrow, red."

I exhaled a breath of relief.

Persistence is key.

A stubborn love

Sometimes we can be so focused on other people and how stubborn they can be that we forget how stubborn we can be ourselves. What makes people so stubborn? Perhaps it's the way we are brought up and how our parents teach us to ignore and move on? Or it could otherwise be an act of dominance in an attempt to not show a weaker side to other people.

I hadn't talked to Casey about his childhood or parents that much since we started dating. When conversations were brought up about our parents, he would often change the subject or avoid. I didn't realise this until Casey returned home from the doctors, like I pushed him to do.

"Arthritis!" Casey exclaimed in a tone of annoyance.

"What?" I turned to enquire more at his abrupt entrance.

"Nothing they can do, April. It seems like my work hasn't been doing me any favours. I have arthritis. It was pointless in me going to the doctors. They can't do anything for me, anyway."

His ignorance about the situation did frustrate me. At least the doctors were able to rule out other possibilities, to provide an answer and recommendations. At least we knew how we could help him, but I knew that this stubborn man would not want to slow down on his work. He won't do what's right to assist with reducing the pain he is enduring.

"It wasn't pointless! At least we know how to give you the best help now," I argued.

I folded my arms as he rolled his eyes, dismissing my comment. He began walking away from the conversation. I couldn't let him. I had too much playing on my mind to let this disappear so easily.

"Why are you so stubborn, Casey?"

My eyes remained fixated on him as he walked away up the stairs. He didn't answer immediately, but he did stop on the step to think through what to say. He made it obvious for me to see through him. I knew he was filtering through words in his head before saying them out loud, to spare my feelings.

"You wouldn't understand," he quietly said, keeping his head down with what appeared to be a distraught emotion playing on his face.

"Casey, please come downstairs. It's time for us to talk, don't you think?" I cautiously asked him.

He knew how communication was the strong point in our relationship. I had opened to him entirely, and I was hopeful that he would likewise be able to find that same release when speaking to me. At that time, I felt as though there was still so much he was holding back, secrets I was yet to discover.

As he stumbled back downstairs like a grounded teenager, I held his head close to my chest, grasping hold of him to show him he could lean on me for anything.

"You don't have to pretend to be the strong one all the time. If it's the way you were brought up to care for yourself, then I just want you to know that it doesn't have to be that way anymore. You have me now."

I needed him to realise that he didn't always have to act like a strong emotional being. He was human too, and I needed him to share with me so I could understand and help him better than before.

He stepped back with a different look, a different side to his personality. His eyes brimmed with water, like a puppy being taken from its own mother and placed in a new strange and frightening home.

"I suppose I never did talk to you about my parents, did I?" He stumbled to collate those few words together and I could already tell by his shaky voice that the mention of his parents pulled on strings inside his heart. Seeing him this way brought me to emotional tears as well, and I didn't even know the full story yet. Rather than using words, I slowly shook my head in response, allowing him the floor to open his heart to me. He needed a listener right now, and I needed to be the one to lift up the anchor from the bottom of the ocean in order for his ship to move on.

"Both of my parents passed away when I was very young."

His face was hidden, trying to hold himself together. His own words were cutting through him like broken glass being repeatedly inserted into his stomach and heart. I wanted to reach out and hug him already, but I knew that by hugging him, he would break down and never be able to finish what he needed to say. He did need to say it. So many men suffer in silence. We all have societal expectations to thank for this. The expectation for men to keep families and households afloat, even if everything else around them is sinking.

"I was only six…" he coughed, trying to clear the emotion from his throat before continuing.

"Me, my older brother, my mum and my dad used to enjoy going to this lake for a weekend walk. We even used to take our bikes and ride around before stopping at a café for food after…" He laughed, thinking back at the fond memories, like envisioning a warm open fire in a house before it loses control and spreads across the room.

"During a very cold winter day, we all decided to take a walk along the lake. It was beautiful, red. Everything was frozen to a crisp and although it was a bitter cold, we didn't feel the numbed pain in our fingertips because we were so excited to go skating along the frozen water."

I watched as his Adam's apple bounced back and forth like a pogo stick that he was unable to put down. He kept shuffling his hands around in between his legs, trying to stay still. I knew that if he managed to still his nerves in his physical appearance, then his emotional state would break through from inside in a stream of tears. The fond memories had suddenly disappeared, and the darkness swept over his mind, taking him back to a horrifying moment in his childhood.

"The water could hold my weight. I slid around the frozen lake with my brother, enjoying the moment. I slid over to my older brother and tapped him on his shoulder... '*Tag!*' I told him, before sliding away as quicky as I could. My brother tried to keep up with me as I attempted to run. My brother stopped and I couldn't understand why. I laughed at the time, but then I watched as my brother looked back at my parents shouting for their help..."

I found myself leaning in, discovering a new man who I thought I once knew.

"*Casey!* I heard my dad shout my name, but I didn't stop, not until I realised that I was creating cracks beneath my footsteps. My dad dropped our bags and ran out onto the ice, pushing me out of the way of the cracked ice and I watched as my dad fell through where I was stood only moments ago."

His eyes became flooded, but he remained looking away from me so that he could steady himself.

"That was the first and last time that I ever saw my dad look that scared. I tried to pull him out, but I was too young and weak. My mum was screaming my father's name, Elijah, at the top of her lungs in pain. She started making her way out onto the ice herself, but it immediately started breaking beneath her weight as soon as she stood on the lake. I can still hear my mum screaming for me to come back before I went in too... I'm sorry, I can't, April."

I rushed in toward him, grabbing hold of his face and pulling it into my chest, holding him close. I couldn't give him any words of encouragement right now. All I could do was hold him tight until he managed to overcome the traumatic recollection in his mind. He has done it once before and he can do it again now. I found myself rocking him back and forth like a mother trying to get her crying baby off to sleep. We stayed like that for a few moments until his cries became silent. I kissed him softly on his head and tried to hold back any tears myself. I needed to be the strong one now.

"I'm stubborn because I had to be my own man as I grew older. I needed to care for my mum before she passed away shortly after. I still believe to this day that she died of a broken heart. My brother never forgave me…"

He stumbled, but he managed to release the most horrific thing that had been tearing away at his chest inside. From here, he could grow again, with me. I still had so many questions, but now wasn't the time to ask. I am the listener and that's all he wants me to be right now, nothing more.

A brew and a red wine-stain

It took several days for Casey to return to his usual self. It was difficult trying to communicate with him over those days, as I knew I was the one to push the fog away to see the clear sky hiding behind. I kept my questions to myself until I knew the time would be right to ask, if there ever would be a time. I was eager to know why his brother would no longer speak to him. I wanted to know how long his father was under the water and how long it took for them to be able to get help. I wanted to learn more about his mother. She sounded like a devoted woman who could not cope without her rock. For now, my mouth stayed sealed.

To my relief, Zeeky had visited during the week to spend an evening with Casey. It was comforting to see Casey being able to laugh again. How I missed that laugh…

I stood in Casey's kitchen, making drinks for the three of us, when I heard a noise approach me from behind. I turned to see a clean shaven, lanky man in front of me.

"Everything OK, Zeeky?" I nervously asked, as he towered over me closely.

"What have you done to our boy?" he enquired in a meddling manner.

"Why?" I refused to answer his question without knowing more.

"Because he's head over heels, talking soppy business about you, red. I've never seen him like this before."

I slowly released a sigh of relief, whilst retaining my composure. Hearing those words brought warmth to my heavy heart. I managed to pull a genuine smile, without the need to pretend to be happy.

I followed Zeeky back into the living room with the drinks in my hands and a tub of Glucosamine Sulphate capsules that I had picked up to assist Casey with his arthritis pain. He had been telling me that the capsules were helping, but he knew that the pain was still there. At least we found something manageable.

"What's this about you becoming all soppy about me?" I raised an eyebrow at Casey as I popped out a capsule from the tub for him.

"I was just saying that it would make sense for you to move in with me. You're here most days anyway and financially it would make sense."

I took a moment to process what he was asking. He wanted to take the next step in our relationship. It made sense, but I wanted my own home to prove to my parents that I wasn't going to rely on another man and that I could care for myself. By putting in a notice to my landlord, will I be showing that I want to rely on someone else again for a joint income?

My heart took over my mind, as I knew deep down that this was right and what I really wanted, not what my parents want from me. I wanted Casey to myself more than ever right now, but I controlled myself, realising our company. Having Zeeky there that day changed my thoughts about Casey's friends, and it made me open my eyes to see the reality that Casey's friends brought balance to his life.

Without further thought, I accepted Casey's proposal. Zeeky jumped up with joy, clapping his hands, showing more energy than me and Casey combined. It was the first time I'd seen Casey smile since he opened his inner demons to me, and it made me feel human again to see the demons leave his possessed body and bring my Casey back to my side.

We all need our friends close by in times of trouble. Sometimes they can open windows that partners struggle to do by themselves.

***

Packing my belongings into two cars was difficult, but I was glad I had Casey assisting me in emptying out my little cottage home. He laughed as he came across old, printed photos of my childhood. I laughed along, as I enjoyed reminiscing about the simple memories. Back then, a problem would be not having enough sprinkles or sauce on my ice cream or having homework to be handed in the following day. Now, the days become increasingly more difficult, especially when I was on my own working through bills and trying to stay financially afloat. Having mechanical problems with my car and making countless trips to the garage.

Trying to please everyone you love just to impress and make them feel proud, but ultimately feeling as though you are failing them. Battling with your own emotions and doubting every single decision you make because you're afraid that it will affect your future.

Things were so much simpler and, as a child, we don't even realise it.

I am still at my happiest though and I learn to appreciate every day. Spending those days with Casey made it easier. Seeing his smile filled a void I didn't even know I had in my beating heart.

"What's this?" I heard him snigger.

Casey's back was turned to me so I couldn't see what he was holding in his hands, but it must have been small. I struggled to answer him, as I wasn't sure myself. He turned, flapping a small piece of paper in the air. My eyes widened as I realised in all my embarrassment what he had come across.

"A receipt for the drinks we had at Moor Café?" His eyes softened so beautifully, and his smile grew. On the other hand, my face reddened, and the warmth built up inside in hopes that he would not read the back of that receipt.

"I keep silly things, give it here," I demanded.

"Oh, but wait…"

No, please save me from the embarrassment…

"A cup of tea solves any issue; I hope you solve the issue of my heart…"

He paused for a moment as he processed my black scribbles on the back of the receipt. I didn't say another word. What could I say that would save me now? Perhaps I could say that it was for a poem, but that sounds like an obvious excuse. I twisted my feet, holding my hands behind my back like a little girl in trouble, using a look of pure innocence to save her from a scolding.

"You know April, I'm like a red wine-stain… I'm difficult to remove."

"I don't want you to be removed," I played along.

"Good, because I'm stained on you forever, red."

"I guess that means you're the cup of tea to my red wine-stained heart, Casey."

A poem made by us in the most unlikely moment.

I helped Casey with the final bags to the cars, but towards the end, I made myself carry more as Casey began hissing in pain again. I made sure he was taking his capsules every day, but I had noticed that he was silently dealing with the pain again. I tried to talk to him about it, but I believed he was afraid to burden me with his troubles after the last time.

Some nights I pretended to sleep, but I could hear and feel him rubbing at his joints as he struggled to get off to sleep.

I hated seeing him struggle and knowing that I couldn't help. I tried researching online, doing all I could to try to help him. I came across some home remedies such as turmeric. It supposedly acts as a good treatment for arthritis. Obviously, it became a no brainer for me to buy these things and mix them in with food to help him, silently.

Maybe his body was becoming used to the capsules? I wasn't sure.

Once we reached *our* home, I unpacked my own belongings into the spare room. I managed to put some of them away, but there was too much to focus on in one night.

After a bath and relaxation, I made my way downstairs to find Casey with his legs up, watching TV. His knees looked sore, but I tried not to draw my focus to them. He already knew that he was in a bad way, I didn't need to add pointless comments to it.

I slumped myself down beside him, wrapping his arm around my naked body whilst kissing him sweetly on the cheek.

"Cup of tea?" I playfully asked.

"No, I think a red wine please, Miss Jones."

I laughed before standing again to reach for the wine glasses in the kitchen cupboard.

"Mrs. April Woods. Sounds made up; don't you think?" he randomly bellowed through the room.

I almost dropped the bottle of red at hearing him mix his last name with mine. It filled me with the same butterflies I felt in those first moments of our relationship and, I didn't want to let go of this feeling. I continued pouring wine into each glass before spinning and dramatically entering into the room. I gave him a cheeky grin that I couldn't hold back.

"I think it has a nice ring to it, Mr. Woods."

"Good," he added. Nothing more, but I did see his facial expression show there were so many more words playing in his mind.

I clinked his glass with my own. "To cups of teas and red wine-stains taking away all of our problems."

He clinked my glass in agreement, nodding his head and pulling half a smirk across his face.

I loved that smirk!

Swans, Sheep, and Otters

As the weeks went on, we managed to give all my belongings a home within *our* home. It felt good to bring our lives together under one roof, and it was made easier when we managed to split responsibilities around the home. If I did ironing, he did the washing. If he did the cooking, I would do the dishes. Life became so simple and although I almost gave my parents a cardiac arrest when explaining the move to them, they had adjusted to the news and became happy for me. I was forever grateful to finally receive their approval, rather than having them fight against my wishes.

Our friends become closer than ever, visiting on a weekly basis for drinks or a movie night. I never felt alone again and having friends join us brought a happy, healthy atmosphere into our already seemingly perfect lives. It became apparent to me that Casey's pain had started wearing off and he became himself once more. I put this down to the weather becoming warmer, ready for spring and summer. The cold was no longer sitting in his bones, and he moved around far more easily.

Either that or he was doing really well at hiding it.

The only thing that was tugging at my strings was his late nights working. Being self-employed, I understood that his income depended on the time he put into his work to complete a project. However, it worried me that he was working such long hours. It also felt as though we could not spend long together before being ready for bed by the time he had returned home.

My overthinking brain did try to sway me into thinking the worst: Has he found someone else that he is seeing whilst I am at home? Is he becoming bored with me and wanting to spend longer hours away from home?

However, I managed to fight back on these thoughts when I would see Casey return home at 7 or 8pm covered in dust, sweaty and sticky from a hard day's work. He would walk through the house and collapse into my hold before giving me the same look that he did when we went on our first date. He managed to complete this with the most intimate entrance - "I love you, red". His words and actions filled me with butterflies every time! I trapped these butterflies into a container, feeding and watering them so they would not leave.

The following Wednesday, I left work and headed straight to the shops to pick up a couple of packs of popcorn for movie night at "J-Dubs". Danny created the nickname a few weeks back for our home. He managed to mix our last names, Jones and Woods, into an acronym. It helped make the house feel like a forever home for me and Casey. It was no surprise that Vanny Danny (lover of Vee-Dub vans) would come up with such a nickname, but we all liked it.

Casey always made sure he would return home earlier on a Wednesday to spend more time with our friends, rather than working until late at night with no life. I just wish he would learn to balance his work life with our life.

"Full house tonight?" I heard my love say, as he walked through the door to be greeted by Zeeky, Danny, Billy and Bernie.

Both me and Casey had started to notice Bernie becoming a little more flirtatious every week with Danny, but we didn't say anything. We didn't want to interfere with nature's course. We watched closely, seeing Bernie slap Danny's leg after he made a joke – Any excuse to be able to touch him.

"Isn't Danny in a relationship?" I whispered to Casey.

"Was…" he corrected me.

I looked up, raising my eyebrows at him in curiosity. Casey turned to look across at Bernadette, narrowing his eyes at her so I would be able to identify who he was referring to.

"I think *she* might be the reason Danny left his partner…" He subtly muttered into a glass, so as not to draw attention. I had so many questions, but now wasn't the right time to be asking when we were only a few feet away from them.

Casey slowly brought the glass away from his mouth and, like a gossiping girl, he leaned into me. "Pretty blonde girl to one side. To the other, a lanky man with a stubbly beard? I think they're a perfect match, don't you think? You can almost hear blondie asking him if he wants another Scooby snack."

I snorted briefly before holding back from further laughter to draw attention. I nodded in agreement, whilst hiding my smile into a glass. I poured back some of the lager to wash away the laughter.

We sat down on the sofa, ready to watch a film together. Everyone had their drink and I noticed Bernadette slowly edging closer and closer to Danny on the sofa. I tried not to look too much, but unfortunately Danny looked back at the wrong time, to see me already staring at him. I smiled in his direction, but it was too late. I watched as Danny scrunched up his face, ready to say something.

Why did I have to give them too much attention?

"Before we press play, I was just wondering how everyone felt about going on a walk through Biddulph Grange Country Park, next Wednesday?"

Thank goodness he didn't ask why I was staring!

"Well weather has definitely picked up recently, so I can't see why not," Casey responded.

"It's settled then, Billy, Zeeky?" Danny turned to them both, awaiting a response.

Both nodded in agreement before we pressed play. Last time we went on a walk in the Country Park, I met with Casey. The nostalgia brought back warm feelings inside me, as I looked admiringly at Casey whilst snuggling under his arm.

I watched Bernie as she eventually lay her head back on Danny. It was funny and relatable to see another fresh, potential couple take baby steps towards getting close with each other. I elbowed Casey gently to get his attention. I felt the chuckle in his chest, beneath my body, as he noticed. He tightened his hold around me and kissed my forehead.

How I loved that...

I decided to take my attention away from the new unspoken couple to stare at the screen and keep focus on the film, as everyone was sitting quietly to enjoy the scenes.

A bright light appeared, causing me to squint my eyes. Loud, unknown noises began blaring, but it didn't seem to be coming from the speakers. In a dark room with only a bright light appearing from the screen, I struggled to identify the cause of the noise. I couldn't see the others in the room, but all was silent, as though they hadn't heard the same noise as me.

My heart rate elevated, and I made my body rigid, reaching back to grasp hold of Casey's shirt, but instead, I felt fur. I turned my eyes away from the light, as my vision adjusting to the darkness and I saw the stag behind me, frantically trying to warn me. I gently held onto the stag's antler, as it guided me through the darkness.

The stag came to a stop and, likewise, I didn't move another muscle.

There's that noise again...

It echoed through what seemingly appeared to be trees. The birds felt threatened and escaped from their nests, flying off into the sky, away from the threat standing on the ground.

Crunch

No quicker did the crunch sound startle us from behind, did the stag gallop forward at speed, trying to bring me along with it.

Bang

I felt no pain but a dull feeling emanating from my leg, making it impossible to move along the ground. Trying to process what had happened, I felt a wet substance dripping down my ankle.

Blood? Where is the deer? Where is the threat?

I collapsed along the sodden floor, grasping hold of leaves, trying to find a weapon hidden across the ground. My heart brought pain to my chest as I felt it beating faster and faster. I clenched onto my chest, jolting back again.

I gasped, looking around me to see Danny, Billy, Zeeky and Bernie sat around staring at me. Casey put his hands over my shoulders in an attempt to calm me.

"Oh red, I think you had a bad dream, are you OK?" Casey reassured me, as I came back to reality.

I still couldn't speak, as I was gasping for air, but I tucked my head into Casey's chest to look away from the stares surrounding me.

The sweet smell of cedarwood on Casey's chest made me feel comforted again.

"Are you OK, April?" I heard Bernie ask, very concerned.

"Sorry everyone, it was just a bad dream. Sorry for ruining the film."

"The film's finished," Billy added with a chuckle.

What? How long was I out?

I looked back at the TV, which was on normal channels, playing through reruns. They must have been talking away as I had slept.

It took me some time to drift off to sleep again that night, as I had startled myself in a very abrupt manner, waking up every part of me... Especially my mind. I wasn't the only one either, as I noticed Casey took some time to fall sleep himself. His eyes were closed, and I could see he was trying to drift off, but he tossed and turned repetitively, trying to find a comfortable position.

I picked up my phone to text Bernadette, in the hope that it may distract me and help my mind to settle from thoughts and be able to sleep.

April: So, you and Danny?

Bernadette: What are you talking about?

April: As if it isn't obvious?

Bernadette: I know. It's nothing serious, so don't overthink it. Anyway darling, I'm going to sleep. Goodnight x

I quietly laughed to myself, before turning to Casey and kissing him on the forehead. I laid my head down on the pillow to face him. I laid one hand over his chest, so I still felt close to him. Luckily, this also helped me to close my eyes and finally bring my mind to rest and sleep.

***

The late nights at work still hadn't stopped and I became increasingly worried when it turned 8:30pm Tuesday night and I still hadn't seen Casey come home. I rang his mobile phone, but there was no answer. Thoughts started playing through my mind, but I tried to brush them away as being silly answers to my unanswered questions. I walked around the house in a repeated pattern. I circled the kitchen, living room, hallway, landing, bedroom, before making my way back downstairs to do the whole process over again.

I sat in the bedroom, staring through the window at the setting sun. It looked beautiful, but I couldn't consider how beautiful the night was with the glowing pink sky, when I had no idea where Casey could be.

I tried to call again, no answer.

I rang Zeeky. Maybe he might know…

"Hello?"

"Zeeky, oh thank God! Do you know where Casey is?"

"I spoke to him about 20 minutes ago and I know he was finishing at work, so I imagine he will be home soon."

"Good to know he's kept you updated, at least. Thanks, Zeeky."

I angrily hung up. How could Casey keep his friends updated, but not his own girlfriend, after I had been trying to contact him for the last hour?

Not long after, I heard the door quietly open, and Casey stumbled in. He looked exhausted, but happy. His happiness made me feel irritated, and I crossed my arms, awaiting answers.

"I know, I'm late. I'm sorry," he said without a sincere apology in his tone.

"Just keep me updated on how long you will be. I was worried sick!" I warned him.

The happiness in his face dropped and he nodded his head, looking down at the floor.

Was this the apology I was after? Because now I feel like the bad guy.

I dragged my feet over to him, wrapping my arms around him.

"You smell like you've been outside and you're very cold too." I held him at arms-length, looking him up and down.

Casey laughed at my strange comment. "What?" He sniggered.

"I don't know how to explain it," I added. "Your clothes feel cold, as if you've been outside for some time and you smell like outdoor trees or something. It's difficult to explain." I dismissed the need for an explanation.

"Well, I have just come in from outside and the smell is probably that Cedarwood shower gel I've been using," he laughed at me, trying to justify himself.

His words still didn't add up to what I could see about him, but rather than making a fool of myself and try to explain what seemed to be a joke, I chose to dismiss it. I felt happier knowing he was safe and at home, at least. Now I could go to sleep in peace.

I began walking up the stairs to go to bed.

"Don't forget we're going on a walk tomorrow, so please don't be late home this time."

"I promise," Casey reassured me.

***

I fanned myself down with my hand, trying to circulate some air around my face to reduce the sweating. Cooking in hot weather with the sun blaring through the kitchen window is not the best condition to be in. I opened the oven door, standing at a distance from the heat, as I pulled the perfectly cooked garlic bread from the shelf. I cut up the bread into slices, putting them beside the pasta dish that I had knocked up as a quick meal before the walk.

I looked up at the clock hanging on the wall, before turning to the front door.

"Come on, Casey," I muttered to myself.

I needed an ice-cold drink. Although, I thought a cold drink would only be like chucking a bucket of water on a burning house with this heat.

I dropped an ice cube into my glass before pouring the lemonade.

My body jolted, almost dropping the bottle from my hands, as I felt arms reach around my upper body, pulling me in closer.

"Hello, beautiful," Casey seductively whispered as he kissed my neck.

I turned to face him, looking at his mysterious eyes with caution. He reached behind, grabbing my glass to indulge in my cool drink.

"Hey, I was about to drink that!" I shouted at him. Before I had another chance to remark on what had happened, Casey pulled me in again, but this time kissing my mouth. It was cold and I felt the ice cube moving around in his mouth, as he charmingly pushed it through into my mouth with his tongue.

"You were saying, red?"

I couldn't talk for the ice cube in my mouth, but even when it would be empty, I wouldn't be sure how to respond. All I knew was that not only was the ice melting in my mouth, but my body was also melting into his magnetic ways. Unfortunately, we had no time to take matters into the bedroom and so I was left with no choice but to frown at him with disappointment.

We walked from the house, as Biddulph Grange Country Park wasn't far from where we lived. It felt enlightening to be able to walk together for the first time in so long. Smelling the fresh cut grass and feeling the evening breeze against our bodies immediately made me feel happier. It is true what they say – warmer weather and walks does help with mental health.

"It's times like this that I wish we had a dog," I hinted into our conversation.

Casey tightened his grip around my hand, looking at me with those soft eyes.

"Are you wanting to take this relationship to the next level, April?" he enquired with those piercing eyes.

"I suppose I am," I expressed joyfully, like a child being promised a new toy.

"Well, what breed dog would you like?"

"Cocker Spaniel!" I bellowed without hesitation and a little bit of spit escaped from the side of my mouth.

Casey chuckled to himself, looking at the joy on my face. He brought my hand to his mouth, kissing it softly. Meanwhile, my mind wandered into an alternative universe on what my life would be like with Casey and a Cocker Spaniel. Casey would say that Lady would need to stay in the dog bed downstairs, but I would sneak Lady upstairs into bed with us, until Casey has to give in. I would learn about all of Lady's funny quirks, and it would bring an abundance of happiness to my life, alongside having Casey there with us.

I was quickly pulled from my trance as I heard our friends up ahead, waiting for us. Bernie reached in, giving me a suffocating hug, as though I hadn't seen her in years.

"We're getting a dog!" I announced to all our friends, without asking for Casey's approval to do so. It fell silent for a moment as they all turned to face Casey for confirmation. Casey shrugged his shoulders while laughing at my unexpected and sudden excitement.

"Well, that's... Big news." Bernie congratulated us both, uncertainly.

I tried to hide my inner excitement for the rest of the walk, as it appeared that my excitedness might have been over the top. I couldn't understand why no one else was likewise excited and rather dismissed the idea of it. Regardless, I continued to think about what life would be like with a dog, and it made me happy once again.

Hearing the running water hitting across the rocks beside us helped relax my mind. I looked up through the trees, as the soft glow of the setting sun embraced an orange glow through the trees. An unusual figurine created a shadowing effect, blocking the sun from passing through. I continued observing the figure, as I slowly started passing the tree.

"Hey look! It's a wooden pair of swans in the shape of a heart!" I quickly tried to catch the attention of our friends. We all looked up in synchronisation, as we appreciated the art sitting in the tree.

"I wonder who made that and put it in here?" Zeeky asked. We all continued looking in silence, as we couldn't understand why it was there, but at least we could appreciate the art formation.

I took a picture on my phone, capturing the glow of the sun pushing behind it. As we ventured around the park, Danny picked up on another wooden animal, hiding in a tree.

"Look over there! I think that's meant to be two sheep?" he questioned.

"It is!" I agreed. "They are holding heads together in the middle… How cute." I took another photo with my phone, but in the corner of my peripheral vision, I caught a glimpse of Casey looking admiringly at my excitement. I didn't look back at him in hopes that he would continue staring at me. It made me feel warm inside, knowing that he loved me for being *me*.

We continued walking around to the lake and my mind was twisting more often than an owl, trying to search for wooden animals, like a child on a treasure hunt.

"There!" Billy pointed up at a shorter tree overlooking the lake.

Two otters that appeared to be holding a box together in the middle. The carvings were perfect, and the detail must have taken the person or even people some time to create and place around the park.

"Hold on!" Casey stopped us all in our tracks. "They seem to be holding something. Let me see if I can get to it."

I watched as Casey began climbing the tree to grab the otters, which were only sat a couple of feet higher than him.

"Casey, please don't touch them," I requested. "Somebody has clearly put in a lot of time to put them around here… For whatever reason."

"Got it!" he declared, holding the wooden figure above his head triumphantly.

I tutted, while turning my head to Bernie, raising an eyebrow at Casey's ignorance. My expressions extravagantly changed, as I was astounded to see Bernie holding her phone towards me while biting her bottom lip to stop her from talking.

Gaining focus on where her phone camera was pointing, I followed it back around to Casey, who was down on one knee in front of me. The box from the otters' paws had been removed and I watched as he slowly opened the lid to show an empty cushion.

My heart was pounding, but also concerned that the box was empty. Casey reached for his jacket pocket as he pulled out a beautiful silver ring and placed it perfectly into the slit of the cushion.

"I wouldn't leave an expensive ring in a tree." He lightened the moment with laughter.

The sliver ring twisted around the edges and joined at the centre, holding a small, petite square diamond. My eyes began tearing up and I held my hands up to my face, trying to tense myself in an attempt to keep it together. My bottom lip started to quiver, and my legs began to buckle beneath my shaking weight.

"April Jones," he began.

I let out a loud, exhaled cry.

For God's sake April! Hold it together… He's only managed to say your name so far!

His eyes softly glowed and he smirked at my emotional outbreak. His warming look filled me with a calming nature again, putting all the seriousness aside.

"April, I want to spend the rest of my days with you by my side. I watch your smile as you look at simple things that bring you joy. You have always had a bubbly heart and you've managed to enclose us both in your bubble, bringing me closer to you. You've made me feel a sense of happiness again, that I believed was to be long forgotten." He paused for a moment, watching as I uncontrollably started crying with happiness and in longing to remember this moment, forever.

"April, will you be my wife?"

Finally!

"Yes!" I swooped in, hugging him tightly, knocking his balance backwards so that I was on top of him. My tears dripped down onto his face as I tried to wipe them away. Casey lifted me back up to a sitting position as he removed the ring from the box and placed it onto my finger.

I looked at my ring in glee. Clenching my left hand tightly, I held the ring close to my chest while looking up at him in complete awe.

"I got it!" Bernie yelled in rejoice. She pulled her phone down below her face, saving the video forever.

"So, this explains the late nights." I finally understood and acknowledged with Casey. He nodded, feeling amused by his own sneaky and clever ways.

"We helped along the way," Danny pointed out, wanting to feel a part of the moment.

My mind become a blur. There was so much I wanted to say and so many ways I wanted to express my feelings. I began realising the time he had put aside perfecting this moment, but it wasn't just this moment, was it? Since the beginning, he has made me his number one priority. This is the relationship that everyone talks about, and I have it.

We stayed by the lake for some time. I remained quiet for the most part, still trying to comprehend it all in my head. We watched the dark clouds starting to blanket over the sky as we stood to depart and return home. My body came to a sudden halt as the others continued walking forward. I turned back to the trees, trying to climb for the other two wooden figures – the sheep and swans. These would be my three sentimental items, taking me back to this exact moment every time I held them in my arms.

I heard my name being shouted as the others realised my disappearance, but I needed to do this one thing first. I ran back towards them once I had my arms full until I heard something move through the trees. The light struggled to show on the ground with the tall trees standing above me and the dark cloud covering over, bringing in night. The shadow ran past me, this time at close distance.

Is that a deer?

Don't be stupid, there aren't any deer in here. I shook my head, trying to bring myself back to reality, before running back to the others.

But what was that?

"We wondered where you disappeared to, April," I heard Casey ask with concern in his voice.

He looked down, seeing his work in my arms, as I held them tight. He appreciatively smiled at me, with our hearts full of love. He took one of them from my arms to make it easier for me to carry them back home. Casey's pace became slower than the rest in front. He wanted to have these moments, just the two of us, in our own bubble. He stopped momentarily, causing me to react simultaneously and face him. His face became ever closer, kissing me on my forehead. I closed my eyes to value his proposed sentiments.

"I meant every word, April…" He slowly pulled away, looking down at me again.

I remember being told somewhere before that if you fall in love with someone, fall in love with their eyes, not the rest of their body. For the rest of their body will age, but their eyes will always remain. I felt entrapped by Casey's green eyes. They portrayed various sensations of wander, mystery, calm and devotedness.

I could always determine Casey's emotion based on his eyes alone. They would tell a truth that his mouth wouldn't. He isn't afraid to look at me and show me his pain or happiness through a simple look alone. He allowed me to look past the forest green to the ground below at the beautiful nature, but also to see the soil below.

When we returned home that night, I sat the swans, sheep, and otters within close proximity along the windowsill in the living room, admiring their fine details. My little assets to bring me a lifetime of happiness.

And I said yes...

I couldn't sleep that night, my eyes welled up with many happy tears as Casey lay there peacefully. I lay on my side staring at him, like a child watching their idol achieve their highest accomplishment. I held his hand in mine, brushing over his fingers with a gentle caress. To no surprise, this man was exhausted from many late nights preparing, but his hard work never goes unnoticed. Should a day arise where I experience dementia, I hope someone I love will remind me of this moment with a swan, sheep and otter.

Loyalty, Achievement, and Luck.

I woke that morning feeling like a fresh, new woman. I inhaled deeply, stretching out my body, turning to Casey to hold him, but his side of the bed was cold. I rubbed my hands over the sheets.

Where is he?

I leaned up in bed, looking around for him but all my senses had been lowered. I rolled myself out of bed, stumbling my way into the landing, yawning loudly. I looked down to see Casey at the bottom of the stairs, appearing to be in some kind of meditation.

"Casey?" I cautiously tread.

No answer?

Without further questioning, I made my way down the stairs to hug him from behind, until I noticed a redness appearing around his knees.

"Your knees look sore…" I pointed out the obvious.

Casey kept his eyes closed.

Is he hiding his pain from me?

"I'll be OK. It's the late nights. I just need to rest," he exhaled from his meditation.

I ran to the kitchen to reach for the tub of Glucosamine capsules.

It's empty? But I haven't given any to Casey for some time. He seemed to have been getting better...

I wandered back into the hallway, opening up our little key cupboard, taking my car keys from their place.

"Where are you going?" Casey asked, troubled.

"To get you some medication," I declared.

I kissed this handsome man on the forehead before leaving for town.

When I walked into Holland & Barrett's, I spent some time looking down the same aisle over and over, for the perfect thing to assist Casey. Perhaps an ointment? Although the Glucosamine seemed to have been working wonders, until it eventually ran out. I picked up a pack of Glucosamine tablets along with a lavender ointment. Lavender is supposed to help calm and relax, right?

When I returned home, I found Casey asleep peacefully on the sofa. I didn't want to wake him, especially if he had a rough night sleeping. I popped out a Glucosamine tablet on the table, next to a glass of water for him, ready for when he wakes up.

Troubled thoughts played through my head. Has he been hiding the pain, rather than talking to me about it? I had never seen him as bad as what I had this morning. I wonder how many other nights he's left the bed, kept awake until the pain passed.

I picked up a blanket and laid it across his sleeping body. My eyes caught a glimpse of the swans, sheep and otters again. I stroked their intricate carvings with my fingers. My deep blue eyes filled like the ocean. The tide was coming in with no control, and I tried to wipe the waves away from existence. I sat appreciating the hours and thought that went into every single one. The months that must have gone into creating these and why did he choose these three animals specifically? The swans, I could understand, they mate for life. The other two baffled me beyond belief.

"Why did he choose you?" I whispered to the wooden art.

"The swans represent loyalty; the ram represents achievement or sacrifice, and the otters represent luck."

I turned to find Casey sat upright on the sofa, downing the glucosamine tablet and water without hesitation.

"You're a clever man, Mr Woods." I smiled at him, whilst still admiring my three wooden gifts of an engagement proposal.

My phone started ringing in my pocket. I pulled it out to see my parents were ringing me.

"Hi mum!"

"Did you say yes?!" my mum says in lieu of 'hello'.

I looked back at Casey, silently questioning him, and I could tell he understood my look, as he smiled and shrugged his shoulders.

"How did you know?"

"Casey asked for your dad's blessing a few weeks ago," she explained.

"Did he now? Well, you'll be happy to know that I did say yes."

"Thank the Lord! You're finally getting married. How was the proposal?"

"Magical, Mum. It truly was…"

I looked back at Casey with loving eyes. I already felt like the Ram who had achieved everything I could have wanted. Casey steadily walked over behind me, wrapping his arms over my shoulders so that his hands rested on my chest. He kissed me softly on my reddening cheeks.

"I will call you back shortly, Mum. I just need to take care of something first. I love you!"

Dad spoke up then. "Okay Goldie! Be sure to call by on us soon so we can see your finger rock…"

"Goldie? Finger rock?" Casey laughed whilst kissing me harder.

"I'll explain later. Now move back to that sofa," I demanded.

Obediently, Casey made his way to the sofa. Sitting upright, he looked back at me with eager eyes.

"Leave the work to me." I made my second demand whilst removing his jeans and throwing them across the room.

I straddled his thighs as his eyes glowed with excitement. Looking down at him, I bit my lip before sinking my mouth on his. My hips moved above him rhythmically, enticing him to grow in a wanting passion. I smiled when I knew I was getting my way. I moved my lips further down his body, in slow repetitive movements, before moving my head back and forth. He groaned out loud in pleasure, while simultaneously filling me with pleasure, knowing he was enjoying the attention. I circled my tongue around playing with him, before taking everything that he could give. I released him and placed myself back on top, while slowly lowering myself. I pulled his hair back in my grasp so that his eyes were looking up at mine. The eagerness in his eyes became clearer as his pupils paced from side to side, absorbing everything happening at once. I kissed him again, pushing myself down, so that I could feel all of him against my cervix.

I moaned, continuing to move rhythmically on top of him. I quickened my pace with him. His eyes began to roll back into a euphoric world. I attentively kept looking down, as I could see he had mentally drifted away into a world of pleasure.

His jade green eyes came back into focus, looking deeply into mine. His eyes narrowed and his bottom lip dropped open. His hands moved to my hips, grasping hold tightly, keeping with my movement.

That's it, right there…

We both groaned and breathed heavily against each other. My forehead met with his, as both of our arms dropped in exhaustion and release. My breasts rested against his chest as I moved my head to rest on his shoulder. Now I was in euphoria, and I didn't want to move away from this moment of tranquillity. Our eyes began to close again, and our breathing started to regularise.

I'm so at peace when I'm with him.

A game of football

The soft orange glow of the sun spread its light through every open space it could find. The transparent glass in my bedroom allowed the sun to pass through, giving a picturesque glow to my magnolia walls. A standing shadow was pinned up against the wall, using the space it had to move around freely. Except when the shadow reached the bedroom door architrave, the shadow broke off, reducing its ability to move forward. It could only move back towards the window, so as not to perish. I gazed at the shape in grief, as even nature could prove that during its happiest and most fulfilling time, it can present just a slight fear of change. Nature always has a story to tell. We just have to listen hard enough to hear the silent spoken words.

I refused to allow nature to decide my fate. I dismissed the shadow by turning away from nature and returning to my folded laundry. I needed to put it away into our drawers before our friends showed up for yet another movie night.

My mind played games with me when I had no one around to talk to. One inconvenience would become a scattered list of petty issues that would build to one huge problem – Is my life just a routine? When nobody was looking, I would look down at the ring on my finger and I would feel a sense of eternal happiness, but mixed with that, I had a sense of fear – What do I do when I am married? Is that it?

I shook my head in disagreement with the second voice trying to disturb my happiness. This is what life is. We have to make our own happiness. There is no end to it, unless we force it to end.

I heard the thankful knock of our friends turning up. I opened the door to see Bernadette and Danny, hand in hand.

"It's official!" Bernie announced before even stepping in through the front door.

I reacted, doing what every female does best in this situation. I created a high pitch squeal only dogs could hear and flapped my arms uncontrollably, before hugging my best friend. I almost forgot about Danny, though.

"Congratulations," I interpreted to Danny, in a much more toned-down manner. Calmly, he responded with gratitude by bowing his head.

"How did it happen?" I enquired, while reaching in the cupboard for a bottle of wine to celebrate.

"During the most intimate moment in Danny's bed, of course…" Bernadette indisputably declared.

I laughed, but I could relate. Intimate times with someone you love can promote oxytocin, creating more prominent emotions of happiness and attachment.

The others shortly followed in, and I could see the brightness in Bernie's face, as she repeated herself to each person as they walked in about their big news. I could see that Casey was happy about the news too, as he brought me closer to him, squeezing me tight.

"How would you guys feel about a football game next week?" Casey oddly interrupted the moment.

"I'd be happy to. Where at?" Danny enquired, with his arm still wrapped around Bernie. I looked up at Casey questioningly.

"Just up the road by the park. The neighbour is trying to get a few people together for something to do."

"Mark?" I intervened, still confused.

"Yeah, Mark has been having a bit of personal trouble lately, so we agreed to do something together. Is that OK?" he looked at me as though I control his every move.

"Of course it is OK," I added. "I just wasn't expecting this, especially with your knees finally recovering again."

Everyone stayed silent for a moment, trying to wonder if this was a small domestic fight that they should be getting involved in.

"What's up with your knees, mate?" Billy asked.

"Nothing to worry about, guys. I just knackered myself from work, but I'm OK now," Casey explained while looking down at me with a message in his eyes asking me not to delve into this any further. I silently agreed and refrained from speaking further on the matter.

Thankfully, the focus of that night quickly returned to Danny and Bernadette. The new, happy couple. Like any new relationship, they boasted about how perfect they were for each other, and I couldn't blame them. They were well suited, and it was nice to finally see a different side to Bernadette. A side that wasn't so hooked up on the single life. Bernadette had achieved so much in her life and as an independent woman, she excelled against the rest. She has had her alone time to focus on being her best self and now she could share new experiences with someone by her side.

I wandered back into the kitchen to grab some more wine. Casey ran his fingers along my shoulders, leaning in for private conversation.

"Please stop worrying about me," he requested with a sincere tone.

"I just care about you," I justified myself.

Casey leaned in, kissing me on the forehead with wholeheartedness.

"I'm your red wine stain, remember? You can't get rid of me. I'm stuck on you forever." He pulled away, smiling, before returning to our friends.

Stop scrubbing to make the stain fade away then, Casey...

***

It was days like this that I enjoyed having a convertible classic Golf. The sun was shining down, without a cloud in the sky. Feeling the breeze of fresh air pushing against my hair felt energetic, as I drove down the country lanes with my mum sat in the passenger seat.

"Is Casey already there?" my mother asked while holding tightly onto her hair to stop it from becoming a windy mess.

"He's just setting up ready for the game," I confirmed, while laughing at the enjoyment of the ride.

I caught a glimpse of my mum looking me up and down. I tried to focus on the road, but I kept turning back to my mum to see what she was focusing on exactly.

"What?" I cautiously asked.

"I've just noticed how much you're glowing recently," she said softly, but somehow also with an interrogating manner.

I scrunched up my face and looked at my reflection in the rear-view mirror. My cheeks started glowing red, but that was with embarrassment that I had someone interrogating me and nothing more.

"I look like me," I said innocently, quickly glancing back at my mother with a raised eyebrow.

"April, are you pregnant?" she asked, with an approach of understanding hidden away within the question.

I laughed absurdly, but hearing the words placed a newfound panic in my mind that I didn't recognise before. I had missed one period, but the contraceptive pill had always made my periods unpredictable. It didn't even occur to me, as I had never tracked my cycle.

As I pulled into the car park, I looked at my mum with worry in my eyes and with honesty pouring out of me. I told her that I didn't think I was.

"Okay." That's all she said before reaching over and giving me a hug. We didn't speak any further on the matter, but my mind began playing 'what if' scenarios in my head. I couldn't even focus on the game as I sat cross-legged with my head resting on my hand. My eyes focused on a dandelion, poking through between the grass, as my mind wandered into another world.

What if I am? Am I even ready? No, I can't be, I'm on the pill… Surely not…

Reality pulled me from my chaotic realm as I saw everyone around me leap forward to run into the game. I started to stand, following suit, trying to find out what was happening. Running into the crowd, I saw Casey in the middle, cradling himself in pain.

"Casey!" I yelped before launching myself to the centre of the crowd.

"I can't stand," he announced with pain and anger in his eyes.

Everyone tried to assist him at once, and Casey flicked his hand up to everyone around, trying to keep them away. I could tell he hated the attention and for people to see him at his weakest.

I knew it was too early for him to play with his knees playing up.

"I think it's broken," he said, trying to remain calm by gritting his teeth together to stop the scream from escaping his mouth.

"Don't be silly," I tried to encourage him. "You just need a little hand getting up."

I pulled his arm around my neck, attempting to lift him. I didn't realise how heavy he was, now that I felt all his body weight piling onto my shoulders. We began slowly lifting until he collapsed to the floor again, with tears forming in the corners of his eyes.

"I can't!" He finally released the pain.

"I'll take him to the hospital," Danny quickly intervened to help.

"No, I'll take him, it's fine," I quickly interrupted. I needed to be there with Casey. I knew the pain he had been suffering from for the last few months and the doctor's recommendations. I needed to be there as his supportive partner.

I looked back at my mum, realising she needed to get home.

"I can take Mrs Jones home, you take Casey," Danny co-operated.

I gave Danny a hug to thank him and apologised to my mother as we separated.

A few people helped bring Casey to my car and lift him into the passenger seat. I held onto Casey's hand tightly and smiled at him to provide comfort before exiting the car park to take him to the hospital.

I've never had to go to hospital for my own injuries before, but I spent a lot of time in the hospital with my grandma, before she passed away some years back. The waiting was long, and I remember being sat in the waiting room with my dad for a number of hours. I used to sit there with a colouring book until my grandma would come out, with more health issues than the previous time we had visited. Then it came to a time when we were sat in the hospital for hours and my grandma never came out again.

This time, I didn't have a colouring book, just an uncontrollable tapping foot and sore fingers from biting. Casey remained quiet but would occasionally grab hold of my hand to stop me from biting down on my fingernails. I noticed his leg had swollen a large amount, but I didn't want to comment. He already knew and he wouldn't want me pointing out the obvious. I was concerned for Casey, but also concerned about myself. I noticed a pharmacy as we walked in. I was tempted to run in and grab a test, but I didn't want to panic Casey. I don't want to cause him to worry when I didn't even know myself.

"I'm just going to the toilet. Text me if you get called in, sweetie." I kissed him softly on the forehead before leaving down the corridor, out of his sight.

I rushed into the pharmacy; I didn't want Casey to become suspicious of my whereabouts. I grabbed a pack of pregnancy tests, containing two, just to be sure.

I locked myself in the toilet, pulling the toilet lid down to rest for a moment, as I read the packet and took out the first test. I wasn't sure why I needed to read the instructions; I knew how they worked.

Let's just do this…

After doing the test, I rested the pregnancy strip on the top of the toilet cistern. I paced around the small area of the toilet cubicle, crossing my arms and tapping my fingers without any rhythm. I made myself go dizzy with thoughts criss-crossing my mind as I paced in a short circle. I looked down at my phone, reading the time.

Why do the minutes take a lifetime when we are in a moment of turmoil?

I sat back down on the toilet lid with my head in my hands, bouncing on the balls of my feet.

Buzz

I pulled my phone from my pocket again, reading a text from Casey.

Casey: I'm just going in now, wait for me in the waiting room.

Okay, at least that will give me a chance to calm my nerves, no matter the outcome, for when he comes out.

It's time...

I slowly stood, turning myself to look down at the results.

Two lines...

I involuntarily began crying to myself in the toilet. How could this be? What do I do? I held myself tightly, squeezing my arms with my fingers to the point it began hurting as much as my emotions. I wanted children, but not now. I'm not ready...

I held the results in my hand, but my hand couldn't stay still. The two lines quickly became four and then six, as tears increasingly poured down my face. I wanted to tell my mum, I wanted to tell Casey, but how? I needed to take this time to consolidate a thought process in my head. I needed to work this out for myself first before telling anyone.

Breathe in through the nose and out through the mouth... And again now. That's it. Calm your mind, April.

There's nothing that can be changed now. What has happened has happened. I cannot dwell on what I could have done, only what I can do now. Everything happens for a reason, and we just need to clear the fog from the path to see why things have panned out the way that they have.

I began creating my own pros and cons list in my head, as I stayed sat on the toilet lid in the hospital that evening.

Pros:

I am in a stable relationship.

We have stable jobs.

Stable incomes.

We have our own cars.

We are financially stable.

We are happy.

We are mature enough.

I have always wanted children.

There that has made me feel a bit better. Maybe it won't be so bad...

Cons:

Casey is struggling to keep up with work, due to the impact it is having on his body. He isn't well enough to care for another human.

If Casey is struggling to keep up with work, this may fluctuate the monthly income.

I would have to take time away from work. Will this affect my career and my goals? Will I be able to stay off work for long, if Casey has to cut back on his hours?

Exhaustion and sleepless nights. Casey is already struggling to get off to sleep at night. Will this cause anger, or worse, arguments?

Will we both experience arguments and take our own exhaustion out on each other?

Will this stable relationship deteriorate?

Now I'm panicking again. My feet are bouncing, and I notice blood around my fingertips from biting uncontrollably.

Breathe in through the nose and out through the mouth.

Okay, let's look at this a different way. The pros I have listed are facts! The cons I have listed are possibilities, probabilities, unlikely events! If me and Casey continue to communicate and help each other, we can make this work.

It is not a baby's fault for parents splitting. If one person doesn't put in 100% effort, the family falls apart. Each party needs to put in 100% effort to make it work. It can be exhausting, but it will be rewarding and full of love.

I grabbed hold of the test, pulling it close to me. I scrunched my eyes shut in prayer. I was not a firm believer, but I could honestly say that praying somehow made me feel better. In that moment, it felt like the time that I broke down to Bernadette, telling her that I had broken up with Matthew. A problem shared is a problem halved. Even though to this day, I still felt like I spoke to myself in that cubicle, it was like a weight had been lifted from my shoulders.

"This is between me and you," I whispered, looking up at the ceiling above me. My words were to go further than the ceiling. I wasn't sure where, but if something / someone could hear my thoughts, they could hear my feelings and reasonings too. This is to be kept quiet for the moment.

I walked out of the toilets, keeping my handbag close to my side. Keeping my head held high, I made my way back over to the waiting room. Casey hadn't come out of the room just yet, but this gave me a chance to steady myself and engage in a normal conversation for when he did reappear.

Hearing the door open, the nurse reassured Casey. "We will just need to wait on the results from the scans, Mr Woods. We'll call you back in once we have reviewed the scan results."

Casey came hobbling over to the seat next to me.

"Well, it's definitely broken. I don't know why they have to wait and review it. It's obvious".

"Just let them do their job." I squeezed hold of Casey's arm, looking at him with sympathy.

"I just don't get it…" He stammered under his breath, shaking his head. "I just simply fell. There was no push or hard surface. I just simply fell." His eyes focused on the flooring beneath us. He didn't look at me once, as he tried to view the moment over and over again in his mind to make sense of it. I wish I could have helped, but my mind was already being torn away from reality. I was trying to comprehend the possibilities of a little part of me and Casey, growing inside.

We were both in our own separate thoughts for almost an hour, before the doctor called Casey back in.

"Can I come?" I requested, with sincere worry for his health.

Casey smiled back at me, holding his hand out. It made me feel warm inside, knowing he wanted me there with him and he wanted me to hold his hand, by his side. I'm not sure if he needed me to hold his hand so I could help him stumble along to the room, but I was there for him, anyway.

Our hands didn't part, as we sat in the two empty seats, awaiting the doctor's results from the scan.

"It is broken, and we would suggest that the cast should remain on for the next 6 – 8 weeks to ensure that it is healed." The doctor ended his observations, but his eyes lost contact with ours, as he looked down at the scans on the table. He seemed to be hesitating to say something.

"I know it's broken. Is that it then?" Casey impatiently questioned.

I could see the anger in Casey building as he heard the news. The anger wasn't aimed at the doctor, surprisingly enough. I knew that he was getting angry with his own body for letting him down and no amount of comforting words would help him right now. I would need to allow him time to adjust and calm down from the harsh truth.

"I will be sending the scans off for further investigation, whilst your leg heals in the cast," the doctor vaguely added.

"Why?" Now I was getting angry with worry.

"We just can't understand how the bone would break under minor circumstances in a field. Mr Woods, you also mentioned how you have been suffering from arthritis for the last few months. We just want to rule all possibilities out."

"All possibilities? What is that supposed to mean?" My voice began to break and for a moment, I forgot I was pregnant.

"Please do not let this worry you". The doctor tried to reassure us both, whilst trying to set realistic expectations. "It's just a protocol we need to follow to ensure all checks have been carried out. There can be a number of different causes for breaks, but our bodies are very good at healing."

We both left the hospital in silence that night. The only noise we had on the way home was the music playing through the speakers in my car. I had so much information thrown at me today that I was feeling mentally exhausted. We both needed time to sleep off today, to start fresh tomorrow and come up with a new plan. I knew that Casey was silently worrying about his work.

When it rains, it pours

Weeks had passed since Casey had the cast on his leg and rather than healing, he felt that the pain was only increasing. I tried to make him feel better by explaining that we still hadn't heard from the doctors. No news is good news, right? I also told him that pain was his body's way of telling him that it is healing. It's just taking its bloody damn time about it.

Isn't it funny how some people can hide away their own worries with a pretend smile, yet they can somehow help someone else move on from their own worries? Every single time I reassured Casey and helped him feel better for a moment, more and more worries built up inside me. I not only had to care for a little human growing inside me, quietly. I also had to help care for Casey around the house, as he struggled on his own. I had to work extra hours to ensure we had enough money to cover bills as Casey had to step away from work for a little while. Casey did still try to do little bits around the warehouse, but he could only work a couple of hours before the pain would become unbearable and he would need to stop.

I started to see another side to Casey in those few weeks. He hated having his independence torn away. He hated that I needed to help him in and out of the bath and in and out of bed. I could understand the frustrations, but I felt like a quiet lamb in the corner, being cast aside from the herd. Now wasn't the right time to share the news with Casey. I wanted to, but not right now. I wanted to tell my mum and Bernadette, but it was only right to share this with Casey first.

It was whilst his leg was still in a cast that he received a call. The phone rang by his side on the sofa. He hesitated to answer at first and looked up at me with wary eyes before answering.

"We would like to arrange an appointment for you with an orthopaedic surgeon, Mr Woods."

My heart sank. I could only imagine how Casey must be feeling. Awaiting a call to confirm it is just a fracture and that the cast can be removed in the next few weeks, had suddenly been cut from the string and dropped to the bottom of the ocean. I tried to remain positive for him. The more I tried, the more the positive bubble started to edge closer to a needle, ready to pop. I couldn't hear the whole conversation Casey had in that moment, as my mind was adjusting to the news of more tests, which could only mean more concerns. I subconsciously lay my hand over my stomach, telling both of us that everything was going to be okay.

I tried to steer away from looking online at the symptoms. Between the phone call and driving him to his appointment, I grew more curious. Pandora wanted to open the box, but she was hesitant at what she might find inside. I shook the temptation out of my head and waited to hear the news from the surgeon's mouth instead.

Casey didn't want me to be there with him whilst they completed further tests and ask him numerous questions. I wanted to be there, but it was his choice and if he preferred to have the tests on his own, then I chose to accept that.

We often take rejection as an insult. In certain circumstances, we need to take a step back to see that we were not told *no* because we were not loved, but because the person whom we love does not want us to see them in their weakest moment. We should not push back on rejection with dispute, but rather accept and comfort them without making our selflessness apparent.

My nights became sleepless and restless, as I had so much cooped up inside that I was unable to express. Some nights I cried silently, so as not to wake Casey when he finally managed to get off to sleep. When alone, I found it comforting to stroke my stomach and talk to our little baby growing inside. As I waited for Casey, I did just that. I was alone in my thoughts, but in my head, I was talking to my baby.

Everything will be okay, you'll see…

"Are you okay?"

I opened my eyes, seeing Casey had come back out. He looked distraught, like the time he told me about his parents.

"Of course I'm okay," I said a little more abruptly than I had meant to. I moved my hand from my stomach and picked up my handbag to leave with him.

"What did they say?" I asked hesitantly, wanting to know the answer.

"More tests and more assessments, that's all," he said with sadness written all over his face and distress in his voice.

"Casey Woods! You tell me the truth right now, otherwise I'll have to storm into that room and find out for myself," I warned him.

I stood straight, refusing to move unless I heard the truth. I straightened my back like a soldier being given orders. As soon as I saw the look on Casey's face, my posture faded and my body slumped, wanting to be apologetic and reach in for a hug. His eyes misted over and, just like the first time I met him, I found Casey difficult to read. His clear forest green had greyed over, and I could no longer see the forest floor beneath the trees. The fog turned to rain as he tried to wipe away the pain.

"They can't confirm, for obvious reasons. They need to send the tests off for assessment, but…" his voice broke.

I watched as his eyes dropped to the floor and he raised the back of his hand to his mouth to stop any noise from coming out. I dropped my handbag and threw my arms around him. I didn't need to ask any more questions. He just needed to know I was there. His cries echoed around us as I brought his face in closer to my shoulder so that he could hide his pain from the outside world.

"For now, we will keep a smile on our faces, okay?" I looked down at Casey, wanting at least a nod as a form of acknowledgement, but there was nothing.

"Worry doesn't empty tomorrow of its sorrow; it empties today of its strength."

I watched as Casey slowly lifted himself from my hold.

"Look at you with your meaningful words. Almost as good as my *don't let the anchor be your burden* saying." He managed to bring out a laugh while wiping tears away. I was happy to see the old Casey again.

"Well, it isn't my saying, but I remember reading it somewhere and it stuck with me," I admitted.

"It's a nice saying, I like it." Casey grabbed hold of my hand as we walked back to the car to go home.

We lay in bed that night facing each other, feeling the same emotion as we did when we first slept together. His fingers stroked my hair behind my ear and his eyes became a clear jade green again.

"You are beautiful," he respectfully whispered to me. His eyes paced back and forth, taking in all my features as a reminder. I slowly watched as his eyes filled with sorrow again.

Is now the right time? Perhaps it will give him something hopeful to think about instead?

I filtered my fingers through Caseys, looking at his hands and kissing his knuckles. He laughed appreciatively. I slowly brought his hand down beneath the duvet and lay his hand on my lower stomach. Casey's laugh stopped at he looked at me inquisitively.

"I'm pregnant," I softly spoke to him.

His expression didn't alter, and his hand didn't move. I felt like Medusa, turning a man to stone with just two words.

Was this the right thing to do?

His bottom lip quivered, and his eyes filled with tears. But were those happy tears or regretful tears? It was hard to distinguish. His hand gently stroked my lower abdomen in a circular motion. Casey's head moved down, and he kissed in the area where our little one would be positioned.

"Well, we're going have to make this work now, aren't we?" He held a kiss on my stomach and didn't move for a few seconds, as I felt his lips quiver against me.

I rested my hand on his head before moving my fingers freely through his hair, trailing my hand slowly down to his arm. I pulled him up from his under arm so that his eyes met with mine again.

"I have a pair of otters downstairs that were brought to life and made with love. They bring all the luck we need for our family."

It is in moments like this that you can truly feel the love escaping our bodies and encasing each other, like wings covering one another for protection. I held onto this moment for as long as I could.

I was preparing myself for anger, frustration, and worry. I was expecting an outburst mid-argument when telling him about our baby. I'm so glad I was wrong. For a short period of time, this news had kept both of us distracted from the pain that the world had thrown our way. This unexpected accident had become our lighter beginning, rather than a depressing aging process.

That was until September 5th…

I still remember the day sending shudders down my spine, like holding a taser gun to myself and being physically unable to let go to stop the pain. All it took was a few short words to change everything we had ever known.

"I'm sorry Mr Woods, but we can confirm that you have osteosarcoma."

I edged closer and closer to the doctor, picking out any positivity that I could. In all of this distress, I wanted something positive to hold on to and encourage not only myself but also Casey, who sat there without any expression showing on his face. A sincere look that almost declared that he had already given up, without first trying. His eyes looked down as he played thumb wars with himself in an aggressive manner. I could tell he wanted to punch the table in front of him, but I would have to deal with distress once we had returned home.

Life wasn't over. The next stage was for Casey to attend sessions of chemotherapy, to try to shrink the cancer and prevent spread. Although aggressive, we still had a chance to fight back. Where there is a will, there is a way… And damn it, if I had to carry the will for the both of us, then that was what I was going to do.

The journey home was silent. I tried to think of the right words to use, but what could I say? I glanced over cautiously at Casey, who I would intermittently see taking a deeply quivered breath while blinking faster and faster to try to fight back the tears. I couldn't use humour as a way to subside the pain with this one. If I reached in to hold his hand, I knew it would break him into a thousand pieces.

My focus was to get us both home so I could hold him through the night and every day and night to come after that. I pulled my car onto the drive and, without saying a word, I opened the door to make my way into the house. I looked back at Casey, who remained seated in the passenger seat, staring down at his knees, his hands clenched.

"Casey?" I whispered.

"Please come inside…" My eyes blurred as I hoped he would acknowledge and follow me into the house, but he didn't.

I walked around to the other side of the car, opening the door and kneeling down to his level.

"April, please don't try using your bubbly nature to bring me in the house."

I didn't respond with words, instead I leaned across him, kissing his forehead while undoing his seatbelt. His stubborn, arrogant personality got the better of him. I threw his arm over my shoulder as I attempted to assist him out of the car to the front door of our house.

"I can walk!" he bellowed with anger.

I didn't rise to his level of anger. Instead, I sat outside my own car while trying to bring light to his darkness.

"My parents once told me a story when I was younger," I began speaking, as his face lifted to listen to me intently.

I picked up a fallen leaf and a stone from the ground, holding them up for visual assistance.

"Life and Death fell in love, but everyone told them they couldn't be together. Life was full of happiness, filling the Earth with new beginnings. Death, on the other hand, took life away with a simple touch. Death became lonely, but Life approached Death with open arms. Death told her to stay away to save her. This did not stop Life from persisting with Death. She would visit him often at a distance to spend time with him. One day Death asked why she continued to persist when he takes away the very thing that Life creates. Life answered Death with a smile and explained that without Life there would be no Death and without Death there would be no Life. Just as plants die back in the winter, they grow to be more beautiful than before when spring arrives again… Casey, I know life has treated us unfairly recently, but with balance and understanding, we can work on this as a team to come out stronger."

I looked back at Casey, hoping for a response. He didn't answer me, but he got up out of the car and followed me into the house. I made my way into the kitchen and switched the kettle on.

A cup of tea will make everything better.

I took the two cups of tea in the living room, but Casey wasn't sitting on the sofa. I stood quietly, trying to listen for rumbling footsteps, but instead I heard uncontrollable, aching cries. I followed the sound into the bathroom, where I quietly opened the door wider to see Casey leaned over the sink shaking at his arms and creating a pool of emotional suffering in the bowl of water beneath him. Seeing him this way popped the positive bubble, that I eagerly tried to hold onto. I stepped forward, resting my hand on his shoulder and rubbing softly, as though my massage would physically ease an emotional pain.

Casey became silent after realising my presence. He tried to wipe away the evidence with the back of his hand, but it was no use. His eyes had swollen up red. His forestry green eyes had become flooded from constant dark clouds covering over him. The salty droplets of rain had seeped past the green forest leaves after holding too much emotional weight and they made their way down his perfectly curved cheeks, to the peak of his chin below.

Men seem to have this inner demon that pushes them to remain masculine in the presence of other people, when all their body wants to do is break down. Sometimes we need a good cry to be able to build ourselves up and move on again. The demon that hides within man doesn't allow them to express this. The grief sits on their shoulders, weighing them down until they cannot withstand the aches and pains anymore.

"I should be the one looking after you and our baby!" he wailed in defeat.

It's just like Casey to selflessly worry over others, rather than himself.

I wrapped my arms around him, allowing Casey to crumble into my arms. I breathed in his scent deeply, holding onto him. I turned my head so that my lips touched his ear to provide reassuring words.

"This isn't a one-way street, Casey. We are both there for each other whenever it is needed. Allow me to help you."

He remained silent, burying his head into my shoulder. I could tell that his inner demon wanted to reach out and tell me I was wrong and that as the man, he is supposed to be there for me. However, his body would not allow him to fight, nor could he find the words to argue. He needed empathy and understanding, and that is exactly what I gave him.

I took Casey by the hand, bringing him back down the stairs so we could sit together and drink a cup of tea. Casey gave in to his bodily needs and laid down under my arm, resting his head on my stomach as we lay across the sofa that night. I watched as he slowly drifted off into a sleep and I ran my fingers through his hair, admiring every little feature about him.

Our minds can play funny games with us. After hearing bad news, we tend to react very well. It isn't until a few hours later that reality will hit us, and our mind will run into overdrive. Our mind will begin thinking about every little thing, causing our heart to ache and become heavy in our bellowing chest.

The hard truth

Nobody prepares you for life's most important moments, not really. It is like a mother sending her young daughter out for groceries for the first time. The mother provides her daughter with an umbrella and some money. She'll explain to her daughter which path to take to get to the store and sends her daughter on her way. Little does the daughter know that as soon as she steps out into reality a gale force wind blows her only protection from her hands, leaving her defenceless… But it's okay, at least she knows how to get to the store.

Nothing prepared me and Casey for our difficulties. What made it even more difficult was how we were to explain to our friends and family without answers to our own questions. Casey and I both agreed that it would be best having everyone come over for the news. Everyone could find out at the same time, and we could work through it together. Nobody prepares you for how sick and mentally drained you feel, the moments leading up to the announcement. I mean, how do you tell somebody that you're about to bring new life into the world at the same time that your own partner is battling daily for his life?

As our friends and family gathered in our living room, finding places to take a seat, we could already tell that they knew something big was about to be announced. Little did they know what the news would actually be. My mum, on the other hand, kept winking at me and smiling. When she knew nobody was looking in her direction, I watched as she sneakily rubbed her belly. Watching her brought a smile to my face, something that I didn't think would come out tonight. *It was time…*

I walked into the room holding Casey's hand tightly, trying to keep a warm smile on my face to save me from breaking.

"As you've all probably gathered, me and Casey have some news that we want to share with you all," I began saying.

"Now, would you like the good news or the bad news?" Casey looked around the room, putting on a fake smile, trying to bring humour to the room.

Everyone looked around the room at each other in utter confusion.

"Just tell us, April," my mum eagerly asked.

I froze momentarily, trying to think of the softest way to go about telling them the whole thing. I clenched hold of Casey's hand tighter for reassurance.

"Well, the good news… I'm pregnant!" I said with an unsure look of happiness written all over my face.

I lifted my hands up for congratulations from everyone and it didn't fail. Everyone stood up to give me a hug and the questions already started – How far along? Were you planning to get pregnant?

Everyone stood up and spoke, except for my parents. They both sat close together on the sofa with concern in their eyes.

"What is the bad news?" My dad disrupted the happy gathering.

I knew that they wanted to be happy for us, but as parents, they also looked out for my wellbeing and wanted the best for me. Due to the fact I started on the good news, trying to sway off from the bad news and put it off for as long as physically possible, my parents knew that it wouldn't be good.

"I'm dying!" Casey absurdly brought the conversation to its knees.

I stared back at Casey with my eyes narrowed in dismay. The room fell completely silent, except for a short burst of laughter from Billy, who thought it may be just a dark joke. After all, it is Casey.

"You're not dying!" I bellowed back at him with denial in my voice. A tear began edging closer to running down my face, but I managed to hold back for a moment. My anger became more visible, as I turned to our friends and family to explain as best as I could and bring reassurance to myself.

"Casey has been diagnosed with osteosarcoma, or in other words, he has bone cancer." The room stared back at me as I tried to think of more words of comfort, mainly for me.

"That does not mean he is dying! He is starting chemotherapy soon and there is a chance we can reduce the size of the cancer for removal." I stared back at Casey as the room still remained silent, unable to answer.

"Casey Woods… That does not mean I am giving up, like you may be…" My eyes paced back and forth, looking for any form of response to ease the pain breaking in my voice.

I couldn't stand looking back at everyone in the room. I knew I was about to break, and I didn't want anyone to see me like that. I straightened myself before pathetically running upstairs, shutting my bedroom door behind me. Like a scolded child, I shut my door with anger and threw myself onto my bed face down, allowing the pillow to absorb all my wailing tears.

Shooting pains fired behind my eyes from my breakdown. The more I ugly cried into my pillow, the more the headache ignited and spread behind my eyes. I tried to calm myself by taking deep breaths, but my overactive mind wouldn't let me, as it kept bringing back terrible thoughts to me.

How are we going to afford the bills? How can I take care of myself while heavily pregnant and also care for Casey? What impact is this going to have on our child? Surely all this stress is going to be bad for me and the baby…

I finally managed to shake away the nightmare thoughts, as my mind fell silent, and I closed my eyes into my pillow. I could hear conversation downstairs. I was happy to know everyone was still here and talking to Casey for comfort. He needed it from more people than just me.

I heard a bang and opened my eyes, trying to adjust to my dark surrounding. I could still make out the colours as the cloud covered over what light there was left. The white egret orchids were in bloom on the ground again, as I knelt down to run their winged petals through my fingertips. A different shade caught my eye line.

"Red orchids?" I questioned myself.

Moving closer, my eyes widened as I recognised blood repainting the white petals. Stained orchids trailed north as I picked my white dress up from the ground to follow it. Something or someone needs my help. I began running quicker before darkness made it impossible. My right foot caught on a mound of dirt, causing me to trip forward onto my arms.

I tried to brush off the dirt and pain to regain strength to move forward again until I realised in front of me lay a stag. He remained on his side, and I could see his belly blowing up and dilating quickly as he tried to keep breathing. I stumbled across to the side of the stag, as he looked me in my eyes, asking for a silent help. I ran my hand across its body to a wounded leg.

A bullet…

I managed to remove the bullet from the wound. I ripped off the bottom of my dress and wrapped it around the wound.

Bang

The stag's ears shot straight up, and I saw the whites of its eyes widening in uncertainty, as he jolted to a stand with a sudden adrenaline rush being injected into his system by fear itself. I held my right arm around his neck to keep him upright as we stumbled on through the woods to safety.

"April?"

I breathed in the scent of my mother's perfume as I came back to a soggy, wet pillow that lay under my face. My mother sat beside me on the bed, stroking my arm for comfort, her eyes also full of tears, as she saw the worry in me. I held myself up in bed, reaching across for a long-needed hug. You can never say that a loving mother's hug does not work in fixing aches and pains, no matter how old you are.

"I was just talking to Casey about different home remedies and food medicines that I can put together that will help him. A dear friend of mine suffered from cancer and they swore by the stuff to help. Casey was up for it. He's not giving up, don't worry."

Hearing her kind words melted my heart and brought floods upwards again as I hid my face in her shoulder to hold it back. My mother ran her fingers through my ginger locks, trying to steady my quick beating heart from pounding out of my weak chest.

"How are you holding up?" she whispered to me softly.

I pulled myself away from her hold, looking her straight in the eyes with a screwed-up smirk to silently say, "don't pretend you don't already know". She laughed for a moment, looking down and holding my hands beside me.

"Me and your father are here for the both of you, every step of the way, no matter how steep this mountain peak is going to get."

"I'll take him for all of his appointments, Goldie." My dad stood in the doorway, unsure whether he should come any closer.

I held my mother's hands tighter and looked back and forth at my parents with blurred vision from what could only be more tears, but this time with happiness that they were there with me.

"Thank you both," my voice broke, but I managed to give my gratitude.

My dad edged a little closer, still unsure. I parted my hand with my mum, waving my arm for my dad to come in and join us. We sat together on the bed, holding each other tightly, not wanting to let go.

"Goldie number two is baking in the oven, then?" my dad playfully added.

I laughed as we all let go from our hold. I looked down at my stomach, while holding my hand softly over my little growing baby. My dad reached his hand out to bring me to my feet. We made our way down the stairs together to find everyone was still around and talking away. Casey looked happy once again, which only brought happiness to me.

Casey took two looks upon noticing that I had come down from upstairs. He pulled me in close, holding me tight and kissing me on the forehead.

"Your parents are amazing," he admitted to me.

I nodded my head in agreement while looking across the room at my parent's making conversation with Bernadette. I felt like a fool, but I'm glad I said what I said. Seeing everyone's support made me understand that we have the best people in our lives. Those that do not give up and will bring light to any darkness.

When it came to everyone leaving that night, Bernadette pulled me to one side, squeezing me tighter than ever before. I groaned at her strength snapping my back.

"Sorry, the baby!" she gasped, pulling away.

I laughed at her naivety before going in for a second hug.

"Seriously now, if you need me for *anything*, you call me!"

I nodded back in agreement at her terms before waving goodbye to all our dear friends and my parents. Before I was able to close the door, I felt Casey's arms reach over me from behind.

"I'm sorry," he muttered softly with his head leaning against my back.

I turned to face him, smiling dearly at his apology.

"From now on, I will be the positive and supportive man that you need in your life. We are in this together." He sincerely promised to me.

"And from now on, more positive thoughts and less crying from me," I promised back.

Our weakness can be twisted to become our strength

Morning sickness began, and it felt like anything and everything made me feel run down. I tried not to wake Casey at early hours in the morning as I sneaked to the toilet to throw up. I began questioning everything when I was on my own.

What if this? What if that? What does it matter? I am where I am now. Stop thinking about what could be!

I held myself still for a moment, with my head buried in the toilet bowl and my hands gripping hold of the edges. I stealthily came to a stand to wash my face before returning to bed. I lay on my side, allowing my eyes to adjust to the darkness. Casey looked so peaceful when he was sleeping. These days, it felt like the only time I would see Casey in a moment of alleviation was when he was finally able to drift off at night. I couldn't let Casey see me struggling through the pregnancy. He needed me more than ever right now, and if I show him even a glimpse of struggle, his guilt would over-power him. I knew that if this was to happen, Casey would refuse to let me help him.

When I woke again in the morning, the sickness had not subsided and a worried sense of me thought that the smell of sick may still be in my mouth. Casey was already awake and getting himself ready for his first session of chemotherapy. My dad had not let us down on his promise and he continued to make sure that he was there, wherever and whenever needed.

Not having the burden of running Casey to and from the hospital for appointments freed up some of my time to be spent at home, doing things I enjoyed. First on my bucket list was to repaint the front bedroom in preparation for the baby. Baby blue is a neutral, bright and happy colour, so I settled on that for the walls. Having things to do also deterred my mind from embellishing on my own painful thoughts and sickness.

My lovely mother had already prepared our tea for tonight, using some of her secret home remedies to help Casey. My mum also warned me about the upcoming days and made me aware of how weak and depressed Casey may become as a result of the chemotherapy. She even went as far as hanging a "dos and don'ts" list on my fridge door:

DO:

Plenty of fruit and Veggies – Greener the better!

Whole grains over processed grains

Vegetable oil only

Lean animal protein / Plant-based protein.

DON'T:

Stay away from fruit juice.

No added sugar

No high saturated fat

Next, she'll be doing a dos and don'ts list for my pregnancy. I would be lying if I said I didn't spend my days searching everything on google regarding pregnancies and cancer. My whole history was filled with it.

My dad returned home later that day with Casey walking in by his side. Both looked exhausted and I knew my dad had missed his afternoon nap, which was very important to him these days. I welcomed them both in to rest on the sofa as I finished off my second coat of paint in the bedroom. By the time I walked back down the stairs, my dad and Casey were lying together asleep on the sofa.

This was one for the photo album...

I pulled my phone from my overalls pocket, trying my hardest not to get paint on my screen before taking a photo of the sleeping pair. I sent it to my mum with the caption reading "I think your husband is sleeping here tonight".

I laughed to myself, putting my phone back into my pocket and made my way into the kitchen for a warm cup of tea for a productive day well done.

***

The days following on became more difficult as we both battled against mental and physical pain. A few short days after

Casey's chemotherapy session, I watched as he collapsed from menial jobs. He became bed-ridden for days without even realising it. Seeing him like this brought pain to my heart, but my mum would keep reminding me that whenever we hit the bottom, things will keep throwing dirt on us. Rather than allowing the dirt to bury us, we must brush it off and stand above the dirt to get out of the hole. At the time, it felt like a digger was unloading dirt into the hole, making it challenging for us to simply brush it off.

Luckily, my parents visited most days, or we would visit my parents for tea. My mum would sneakily add in spinach or broccoli into meals, trying her best to help Casey through the tough times.

"Won't be long until you'll have your 12-week scan now, April," my mum excitedly brought up.

I nodded, whilst flushing the food down with a pint of water at my parent's dinner table.

"That's right. Casey is looking forward to it, aren't you?" I looked to Casey so he could become involved in a positive conversation.

Casey smiled and grabbed my left hand, twirling the ring around on my finger.

"Our little family," he laughed through his nose while staying focused on the ring. "I was thinking, you know; we should bring the wedding date forward."

"Why?" I asked him, worried about what his response may be.

"I think it would be lovely for our baby to be born into a life with a married couple." He answered with sincerity, but somehow, I didn't believe that was the only reason.

"Wow! That soon?" I looked at him to see if he was sure. He nodded silently.

"Casey, I'm already 10 weeks pregnant. My dress would have to be fitted for a heavily pregnant belly. We would have to be married within the next 30 weeks for that to be even possible."

"But it is possible," he concluded the decision.

My parents agreed with Casey, but my mind started worrying about all the planning, the dress size, the bookings... We don't even have a venue in mind! The one thing that topped all of this was the thought that Casey was bringing it forward for a different reason. Rather than fighting this with him, I chose to let it go and agree with him. The more I wanted to fight against this, the more I knew Casey would begin to panic and become withdrawn. I couldn't do that to him right now.

"This cancer has made me realise how precious life is and how to spend it wisely. April, I'd marry you tomorrow."

Without sounding like a broken record, every single time this man expressed his passion for me, it made me melt into a thousand romance sonnets. Each sonnet had its own important message that could not be left to be forgotten. Simple, meaningful words is all it takes to show someone your true feelings.

How could I say no to him?

Two tiny hands

A plum. That was the size of our little baby as we looked at the screen, pointing in awe at those tiny little hands covering its face from our vision.

"It looks like your baby is playing peekaboo," the sonographer teased.

I grasped hold of Casey's hand, squeezing tight. I didn't dare look up at Casey, as I could feel tears of happiness welling inside, ready to burst out at the sight of our own darling, growing inside. I knew that one glance at him and I would break upon seeing his face of happiness as well. Instead, I bit my knuckle, trying to hold back my emotion, staring at the ultrasound image.

We were overjoyed at hearing that everything was going well and that I should continue doing what I was doing. Little did she know that I was under a vast amount of stress at home, and I had concerns about this impacting our baby's health. I tried working on this myself by meditating at home and remaining positive, as Casey was still going through treatment and becoming more and more exhausted every time.

I felt like my life was spent around working and appointments with very little time in between to relax. I was so grateful for our friends and my parents helping out where possible, but it didn't stop the fact that inside, Casey was battling a war against his own body. He was trying to keep a smile on his face, but I could see past the fake smile. Inside, Casey was holding a blade up to himself as a threat to scare his own demons away. To this day, his threats were not working, and my fear was that he would no longer use an empty threat, but act on it in a literal sense. With no Casey, there would be no demon to take possession of his body. However, that demon would find a new home and torment those closest to him.

During my twelve-week scan, I managed to temporarily push these thoughts to one side, as I had something so real and fulfilling to maintain and stay joyful about. Little did this plum realise how much it was impacting my life and my stability without even seeing it in person, yet.

"Until we know its gender, I think we should give it a nickname." Casey stroked my stomach on the journey home, as Bernadette had offered to take us to the hospital and drive us home after.

"I think Baby Bernie is a good name," Bernadette joked.

"I was thinking Woody," Casey said with no humour in his tone.

Bernadette snorted at the suggestion, before stopping to ask, "like Toy story?"

"Yeah! Well, Woods is my second name and Woody reminds me of my favourite Pixar movie. Quite fitting for a baby nickname, I think."

I giggled at his explanation, but held his hand over my stomach, nodding my head in agreement. Bernadette looked back at me in her rear-view mirror, shaking her head with a smile on her face. I smiled back with a subtle shrug.

Bernadette pulled the car up outside our home. I leaned over the centre console and hugged Bernie from behind.

"I love you both," she said sincerely, as Casey exited the car.

I remained in the back seat, holding eye contact with Bernadette in the rear-view mirror again.

"Would you be my maid of honour at my wedding?" I asked.

Bernadette shot around in her seat, facing back to me. She stalled her car in the process, realising that she left herself in first gear when receiving the surprising question.

"Women!" Casey chuffed from outside the car.

Bernadette took no notice of the comment, as she was still processing what I had asked.

"Yes! Yes! Yes! I love you!" She merrily accepted.

I gave Bernadette another long hug before getting out of the car to make our way into the house. Me and Casey still had so much to plan with the little time we had.

"Cup of tea?" I asked, as Casey slumped himself down on the sofa.

"I just need a rest, red." He collapsed onto his side in exhaustion.

I flicked the kettle on and made my way over to the wooden otter sculpture that Casey had made for the proposal. I opened the little box and pulled the 12-week scan from my bag. I kissed the little face covered by two tiny hands before placing it carefully into the box. My little keepsake.

"I think we should have an evening meal somewhere, red. We need at least a couple of normal moments in our very abnormal life right now."

His eyes were still closed as he hugged the throw tightly around his body to stay warm. I smiled at his good intentions to keep our lives normal and happy, even in the bad times. I approached him quietly, so not to disturb him, and kissed him gently on the forehead.

"How about The Stables Inn, tomorrow, 7pm?" I whispered to him.

"I'll be there. Do you need picking up?" He laughed at his own incapabilities, without opening his eyes to look at me.

I pulled half a smirk and looked at him with wandering eyes. I couldn't see it until now when I looked at his body closely. His jawline was more pronounced, and his body looked frailer. The man who could work so brilliantly with his hands now looked as though he couldn't hold a hammer to a nail. It is difficult to see somebody you love suffering from chemo treatment, knowing that it is the best thing for them, but seeing how it affects them both mentally and physically. I leaned down and kissed him again, before heading to the kitchen to book a reservation.

The hidden truth

I walked down the narrow cottage stairs, holding onto the railing, as I took each step with caution. Casey's eyes met mine at the bottom of the stairs.

"You look absolutely ravishing, red," he gleamed with joy whilst watching me take steady steps towards him.

I decided to wear my pistachio green shaded dress. The material managed to stretch over me, revealing my growing belly. It was not completely obvious that I was pregnant, and I grew concerned that people may think I had a potbelly. I didn't want to hide my little treasure and chose to flaunt our little gift. I held a white purse in my left hand, which matched my white flat dress shoes.

He held out his hand, allowing me to step by his side at the bottom of the stairs.

"I'm guessing I can get drunk, since you're the taxi driver tonight," Casey joked again at his own disadvantages.

I drove us through Derbyshire's beautiful hills and setting sun as we made our way to The Stables Inn. It was a beautifully extended pub that had views for miles. I used to envy the people who lived in these areas and woke to see nothing but nature in all its beauty. However, I then realised that it would be like Christmas every day. Everything surrounding would become normal and a routine. At least visiting every so often, I can feel the same shimmer of peace inside, every time I looked out through the rock formations and heather hills.

I assisted Casey out of the car, even though he waved me off to tell me he could do it alone. I wanted to help him, but his stubborn nature made it difficult to do so. At the door, we waited to be seen. A young girl with her tied back brunette hair approached us. She was chewing loudly with gum being stretched between her teeth. I watched as she looked Casey up and down with a mischievous smile. I coughed to get her attention, and her smile soon disappeared as she came into contact with me.

"A table should be booked under the name of April," I stated, without a polite introduction.

She continued chewing disturbingly as she looked through the reservation book. Her eyes slowly came back to mine, and I watched as she opened her mouth slightly, showing her gum being tossed around by her tongue to the other side of her mouth. It looked like a washing machine on a whitewash. The gum went to the back of her molars as I watched her chomp down again. The more I tried not to look, the harder I found it to turn away.

"Just over here, Mrs Woods. Follow me," she looked disapprovingly before turning back to Casey with the same inviting smile.

I followed her closely to our table when I felt Casey's hand tap my shoulder.

"Mrs Woods?" he elatedly asked me.

I smiled to myself and leaned my hand back to hold his. I squeezed it tight as we continued through the room to our table.

The loud-mouthed lady turned to point us in the direction of our table for the evening. Casey overtook me and pulled out the chair for me to take a seat at the table. Disregarding me completely, our waitress turned to face Casey with a glow in her eyes as she handed him the menu.

I couldn't see her face, but I could still see the bottom of her chin moving up and down irritatingly as she spoke to Casey.

"Here is our drinks and food menu. Unfortunately, the Chef's special pie is no longer available. I will give you both a few moments to read and I'll come back to take your order. My name is Chelsea."

Of course, it was Chelsea. It is such a sassy name. I didn't need to see her face to know she was flirting. I could tell just by the way she spoke to him softly, right whilst I was there in her presence. She spun on the spot, turning away from the table, swaying her hips for Casey.

"My name is Chelsea," I mimicked while making my tongue clap at the bottom of my mouth. Casey held the menu up to his forehead, laughing behind it.

As promised, Chelsea returned to us only a few minutes later with a pen and paper to hand.

"What can I get for you handsome?" she asked Casey whilst again turning her face away from me. Her attitude and flirtatious behaviour began to infuriate me, especially as she continued chomping away on her gum. Casey ordered for us both and I watched as Chelsea took a step back, biting her bottom lip. She wrote the final dish and looked back to Casey, giving him a wink.

"Oh, Chelsea?" I called her back as she started to walk away.

The waitress turned around again to give me a further disapproving look. God forbid I was to ask for something else.

"If you're exercising your jaw for a man back at home, I would recommend less chewing and more sucking." I smiled innocently back at her.

I watched as her reaction satisfied my hopeful response. Her bottom jaw dropped open, showing her gum hanging from her top molars. She became speechless before straightening herself and with her head held high, she stormed off to the kitchen. I looked back at Casey, who had his head in his hands in hysterics, trying to subtly hold it together.

Casey looked back up at me with his face as red as my hair.

"Expect your drink to have her gob in it," he warned me.

"I wouldn't be surprised if her bottom jaw is still dropped open and her gum falls in my drink," I added.

Casey folded his top lip over his teeth, trying to hide an obnoxious laugh. I missed his laugh and his smile. I don't see it nearly as often as I used to.

Our drinks were brought by a young waiter this time. He placed our drinks down on the table and remained professional with us both.

"I would just like to make you both aware that we will be having a live singer tonight at 9pm, should you wish to stay," he smiled at us both. We thanked him for his kind service before he left again.

"Would you like to stop for the singer, or has Little Miss Gob put you off?"

I smiled again and I was grateful to hear he wanted to stop out and enjoy time with me where we can both be normal for once.

"I'll just have to make sure Little Miss Gob doesn't do the slut drop in front of you during a dance," I playfully added.

Our night continued to be full of laughter and I was absorbing every single moment. I never wanted it to end. Not for one moment did our personal problems come to mind. It was a short-lived moment in the long scheme of things, but it was a moment that I could always remember and hold on to dearly.

At 9pm exactly, the young male singer stood in a corner with his microphone and an organised Karaoke version of songs to play through until midnight. His starting song was *Rock around the clock* by Bill Haley & His Comets. The starting song set such a lively climate for all the customers and staff there that night. With such a strong start, we could only hope he could continue with the same energy through the night. As the song list continued, the young singer slowly worked up through eras from the fifties.

At first, I was sat cross-legged in my chair clapping my hands together in time with the music. Casey kept looking back at me with admiring eyes. I watched as the singer grabbed a blue microfibre towel from behind him, as he wiped the sweat back, making his black wet hair become swept back to look like an Elvis impersonator. He went onto his next song, which was *Joy to the world*. Casey watched the singer with his back facing me, so he could enjoy the entertainment. Without looking back, Casey reached out for my hand, which was lying on the table. He squeezed it tight before turning to me. His eyes lit a bright emerald green.

"Care to take this dance, Mrs Woods?" he asked with the brightest smile I could last remember on his face. I gleamed with happiness and rose from the table to make way to the open space on the floor.

Casey didn't dance well, but that's what made it even more enjoyable. We weren't there to impress, we were there to live in the moment with each other. We didn't return to our table, except for a drink break. Our eyes did not look away from each other, as we laughed at our hilarious dance moves that sometimes weren't even in time with the music. Slowly, other people began to join us on the floor as we danced the night away.

That was until *Baggy Trousers* by Madness played. I watched in fascination, as he knew all the words off by heart and could keep in time with the music, whilst swinging his arms and legs back and forth. He began to get out of breath and, obliviously, I put his exhaustion down to the song itself. That was until it got to the second verse, and I watched as his arms and legs stopped swinging and Casey grabbed hold of his t-shirt, putting pressure against his chest. His smile disappeared and his eyes looked straight through me before rolling back. His body mirrored his eyes, falling back to the floor.

Like my dreams, I found that for a moment, I couldn't move. I couldn't understand what had happened. I felt like an old VHS tape that had begun glitching and freezing. All you want to do is hit the side of the TV and tell it to work again and after a few moments, the film proceeds to play. My brain was trying to send all the right signals to my body to move, but for a few seconds, my body couldn't decipher the message from my brain.

After a few seconds, I dropped myself down beside Casey. I held his head on my lap and his hand was held tightly to mine. Tears fled from my eyes as I begged him to come back to me.

"Casey, please!" I screamed.

"I'm ringing an ambulance," I heard a man shout from behind. I didn't look at the people around us, I just kept shaking Casey's hand, begging him to look at me again.

How could I be so careless? I knew that this would be too much for him. Why didn't I think? Because you're stupid! That's why, April. You're just a stupid woman!

I scrunched my eyes tightly shut, forcing a headache. As we waited for the ambulance, I kept checking Casey's breathing pattern. For a few moments, I was certain he wasn't breathing, before he suddenly gasped for air. His lungs sounded like he was full of a chest infection. The ambulance was only ten minutes, but it felt so much longer as I delved into dark thoughts.

Casey was rushed off to hospital that night and I followed as quickly as I could in my car. My legs were shaking as I struggled to drive in my classic car. My gears would grind, as my shaky left leg could not operate the clutch properly.

I was not allowed in the room as the doctors flooded in to assist my husband to be.

I sat waiting, blaming myself for everything. After what had felt like days of waiting, I was finally met by a doctor, who left the room with what appeared to be a forced smile.

"He will be okay," he gracefully opened with.

A sigh of relief left my lungs, before preparing myself for more news, which may not be as fulfilling as what I had just heard.

"His lungs have had a build-up of fluid, and we are now draining the fluid from his lungs. Unfortunately, as Mr Woods treatment has stopped, his cancer is growing more aggressively and is affecting his capabilities. We would highly suggest that Mr

Woods refrains from a lot of movement, especially since he is now in palliative care and the treatment has stopped working."

A moment of silence clouded over me as I replayed those words back again in my mind like rewinding the VHS tape past the glitching to hear the words more clearly.

"I'm sorry… The treatment stopped working?" I questioned him.

The doctor looked hesitant and cautiously proceeded to speak to me as vaguely as he could, unknowing of how much I was already aware of. His mumbles and stutters became a fog in my mind and as much as I needed to hear what he had to say, my ears became blocked from passing the message onto my brain.

The voice had stopped, and I regained focus, looking back up at the doctor, who looked more nervous than ever.

"Thank you," I mumbled whilst turning my attention from him to the floor.

The doctor took one step back and stopped, in case I needed anything further. After a few moments, the doctor turned again and returned to his work.

When I was able to see Casey again, I entered the room with a smile stuck to my face, hiding my pain from him. I sat down beside him, stroking his arm for comfort. Our newly introduced normality shot back to me as I looked down to see needles and tubes being stuck in him.

"I'm so sorry." I broke.

I heard his heart rate monitor increase slightly, as he asked me why I was sorry.

"I should have known better. I shouldn't have let you dance for so long. I should have been there for you."

Casey's heart rate began stabilising again as he gave me a reassuring look.

"Tonight, was the most fun we have had since finding out about this whole shit show. I am not sorry about it, and neither should you be."

I raised my head, smiling at him intently. He was right, of course he was right. I looked down again at his chest as I watched him breathing again. It took me back to earlier that evening when I was panicking that he had stopped breathing and gasping for air. I thought I was going to lose him.

"Why didn't you tell me that you stopped treatment?" I mumbled whilst still focusing on his chest.

Casey didn't speak at first and I listened as his heart rate began increasing again. Upon realising what I had asked and the situation we were currently in, I looked back to him with a reassuring look, as if to say, "I'm not angry".

Casey's head dropped in self-disgust, before being able to put the right words together for me.

"Your dad brought me to another appointment, where it was explained to me that the treatment I was receiving was not working. Apparently, the tumour contained molecular changes, which made my cancer unresponsive to the treatment being provided. In other words, red, my cancer is just spreading and growing more aggressive."

He stopped for a moment, but I knew he wasn't finished by the way his eyes narrowed. I knew he wanted to make sure I was following what he had said so far.

"I'm sorry I didn't tell you sooner, red. I really am. I asked your dad not to say anything because I wanted to tell you for myself. Now I've left it too late. I'm so stupid!" His teeth gritted together with anger and his heart rate increased again.

I softly shushed him and reassured him again with a gentle touch. I wasn't angry, just upset.

"April, I'm the luckiest man in the world, and I can't wait to marry you… And I promise, I'm going to stick around long enough to see our little one grow."

He tried to turn his body to lean further into me, but his teeth ground together, trying to push through the pain.

"Casey, don't put more stress on your body. Please rest." I stood to move closer to him, so he didn't have to struggle to move closer to me.

"I didn't know how to tell you, red. I wanted to avoid as much stress as possible while you're pregnant."

My eyes began to flood, but this time they were flooding with gratitude for this man.

"Hey, April?" he modestly asked.

My oceanic blue eyes flooded, filling his forest green eyes with water for growth.

"I'm your red wine stain, remember? I'm going to be stuck around for a good while yet. Nobody is getting rid of me that easily, not even cancer."

The bells are ringing

I saw a light begin to rise through the solemn trees. I had been trembling for what felt like hours next to the stag. Every few steps, I would hear a groan as he pushed on through the pain to walk to safety. I looked down at my once white dress, which was not visible in the darkness. The deep red stains covered the dress like a paint brush being dipped in paint and swung back and forth deliberately to create a frightening effect. This was real, though. The longer I looked down at our trembling feet, the more the blood soaked up from the bottom of my dress.

The trees bled out sap from their trunks, as if it was mourning our presence. The dry wind blew through my fingertips, causing the blood to dry and become sticky and unbearable. Will I ever be able to remove this from my body or even my memory? Will this torture me for my remaining days here?

I began feeling a dull pain in my chest. I pressed my bloody fingers to my heart and as I pulled away, a new stain began to circulate the area. My breathing became ragged with panic. I wasn't shot, yet my heart was bleeding out in pain. I pulled my right hand away from the stag to steady myself. The stag looked back and called out in pain upon noticing our combining injuries. I tried to look at him, but my vision blurred. The wind stopped breathing for a moment, as I quivered around on the spot to stay conscious. The wind needed to exhale and, upon pushing a gust against my body, I fell backwards, allowing gravity to lead me to my fate.

I took a deep inhale and jolted upright, looking around in my old room. Instinctively, my hand went straight to my belly, where I felt my baby boy sitting quietly. At 28 weeks, there was no disputing that I was pregnant, and it filled me with joy knowing that a part of both me and Casey was developing beautifully.

I swivelled myself around in my bed, making my way through the room to the bathroom.

"Cup of tea, love?" I heard my mum shout up the stairs to me.

With a mouthful of foamy toothpaste, I attempted to shout back a 'yes' to her. I looked at myself in the mirror, thinking about how much needs to be done this morning before the big moment. My mum sat with me last night, putting my hair into curlers, making it easier to style this morning. My eyes looked baggy from exhaustion. Wedding planning, pregnancy and a terminally ill partner are not the easiest combination to deal with. Regardless, we all keep our heads high and full of positivity.

I spat out my toothpaste into the sink and returned to stroking our little baby boy.

"Daddy promised he will meet you and I can't wait for the moment that we both do, little one."

My father stayed sleeping while me and my mother rushed endlessly to make sure everything was visually perfect for my wedding. I sat in front of my standing mirror in an old turquoise wicker chair. My mum removed the curlers from my hair, revealing a new beautiful style.

"There's some fraying frizzy strands that must have fallen out in the night," she grumbled to herself. She turned to grab a bottle of something from behind us to calm the frizz and keep my hair intact for the day.

Using flower hair pins, she pinned my hair back out of my face. I could feel myself drifting off slowly as she applied makeup to my face. It was unusual to feel this relaxed these days, but I enjoyed every moment before I was about to go into panic mode again.

"Now the dress!" My mum clapped her hands together with excitement. Her words alarmed me, as I brought myself out of a light sleep to look at my makeup in the mirror.

"It's beautiful!" I admirably applauded her talent.

With a bit of extra help, I managed to fit into my white empire waist dress that complimented my pregnant figure beautifully. I held onto the bottom drop, bringing it up a little higher in order to spin slowly and watch it sway around me. I tried to hold back the emotion after just having my makeup applied, yet upon seeing my mum's face, it became more difficult to hold back my happy tears. My mum's hands were held together in a prayer like motion, bringing them up to her mouth, trying to dig her teeth into her knuckles to stop the crying.

"If you cry, I cry!" I pleaded, before running into her hold.

"Don't wipe your makeup on my shoulder," my mother warned, while simultaneously managing to deflect the emotions from becoming too much before the wedding itself.

"Another cup of tea!" she insisted.

While walking down the stairs to the kitchen, my mother shouted to my father, requesting him to start getting ready. After all, he needs to walk me down the aisle and God forbid he looks a state while everyone is staring at us.

The finishing touches were complete and without blowing one's own horn, I felt like a million pounds. Every time I saw myself in a mirror, I had to stop to ask myself if that was really me. Rather than looking out of place, having a pregnant belly in a white wedding dress made me glow. It wasn't often that I could see myself with that mentality, but this was all thanks to my mum's hard work.

An old sounding horn blared down my parents' drive. Luckily, we didn't have neighbours close by that would be disrupted by such an extravagant noise. The window slowly rolled down to reveal my dad's old friend in his blue Chevrolet Bel Air.

Throughout planning for this day, my parents have helped in every way possible to ensure we can have our wedding brought forward. Through people they knew, they managed to pull together the unique day. Luckily for me and Casey, it also worked out to be a lot cheaper than we anticipated.

"Brian!" my dad called, walking out of the house to greet his old friend. Even though they don't see each other often, they still approached each other like not a day had been missed.

My dad stood outside for a while in his 'old but very special' navy blue suit. His trousers looked like they were one

Dorito crisp away from popping open, but he loved that suit and couldn't part ways with it. A white handkerchief was folded neatly in his suit pocket; probably my mum's doing as well.

My mother had spent so much time taking care of me and my father that she still needed to get ready herself. I could hear doors slamming upstairs as she tried rushing around to make sure she looked perfect for her only child's special day. I made my way up the stairs and saw my mum grasping hold of her hair, trying to hold back from ripping clumps out.

"Mum, let me help you," I insisted.

She immediately released her hair, looking up at me apologetically for her anger.

"I haven't got time to style my hair," she panicked.

I sat my mum down at her dressing room table. Looking at her in the mirror's reflection, she looked back at me with proud eyes. I felt myself welling up inside, so I broke the connection by blinking away the wet eyes.

"You work on the makeup; I'll style your hair," I commanded.

She puffed out a short laugh, before grabbing hold of her eye shadow palette.

After about thirty minutes of styling, we made our way downstairs; my mum holding the bottom of my dress high enough so that I would not trip. Slowly walking down the drive, we were met by the dropped jaws of my father and his friend.

"You can't outdo your own dad with perfect looks, but you've both done a bloody good try." My dad tried to use humour as his way of avoiding an emotional cry and every time it worked.

I went in for a hug; the side of my face squashed against my dad's chest. I held onto him one last time, before I changed from his family name to become Mrs Woods.

It didn't become any easier when my dad walked me down that aisle, his arm hooped into mine, pulling and squeezing tight. His touch was like a reassurance that no matter what, his arm will always be there for me to hold on to and pull myself back up.

The moment following that walk came the biggest decision of my life up until that point. Some may think the baby was the biggest choice, but that was an unexpected miracle. It was not planned and, upon finding out, the decision was already set in stone. Whereas, this moment, I could still walk away, if I wanted. This is the moment that I choose to give up my family name, give up my family home. I have chosen to accept this man and every single little thing that comes with him. It was the biggest decision of my life to date, and I was all in without a doubt in my mind.

Casey's best man, Zeeky, assisted Casey out of his wheelchair to a standing point, upon noticing my arrival. Casey's legs trembled at first, as I could see he was pushing aside the pain. The medication had stopped working, leaving a weak body to fend for itself. The only push to go on was his brain telling him to do so.

Whilst I was gaining weight to only just fit in my dress, Casey's recently fitted tailored suit was already becoming baggy on his slender body. He stood with confidence, looking down at the floor, before turning to watch me walk down the aisle slowly. His right arm sleeve wiped away the tears falling from his eyes, and he looked at me with that same flattering smile that I always remembered. The same flattering smile I saw when he first glanced at me on that fateful evening.

Believe me when I tell you that this is a scary moment, and my body trembled during the ceremony. Not because I doubted us for one moment, but because I had to repeat "until death do us part". Those five words tugged on my heart, like a child pulling too hard against the strings on a delicate harp. Death will not be our reason to part. No, death will be our reason to hold on even closer to our feelings and memories. Retelling stories and holding on to his belongings for comfort. I would not part ways and I refuse to believe that.

I am not naïve, I know that I would eventually move on, but I will always remember the joy and love I held dearly for this man. That is not something that death can steal away from me.

In those few moments, I imagined sitting with our little boy and presenting him with albums holding pictures of his dad. Telling him stories and encouraging him to fight on, just like his father did.

Casey might not be here for as long as I would pray for, but his imprint on our lives could still have an everlasting effect.

An effect to encourage others to be like him, and who wouldn't want a life with a Casey Woods in it?

"I do," I announced for all to hear and rejoice for our joined marriage.

Following the ceremony, we all made our way to a quaint area in the Derbyshire countryside. A venue chosen specially by me and Casey. Within the hills and trees sat a country house with plenty of parking and a large barn, specifically used for special events. Rather than chairs, they had hay bales for guests to sit on. They used white linen, wrapped into the shape of twisted rolls. Twisted within it were fairy lights, making a soft white glow. As the night went on, the lights looked like fluffy clouds that had been lit up.

Danny and his girlfriend Bernie (it's still weird saying that) managed to speak to a friend in a tribute band to play for us on our wedding day. I listened to a few of his songs before the day and I enjoyed the music. To my astonishment he really outdid himself on our wedding day. I was sure that the only reason we managed to pull everything together in such a short space of time and minimal budget was just out of sympathy. I was grateful for it, I really was, but I didn't want to seem like a spoilt child using life's challenges as a means of getting exactly what I want. Due to that, I wasn't truly able to relax on our wedding day and I found myself trying to greet and thank every single person that showed up on our special day.

Billy held my shoulders at arm's length away, looking at me with concerned eyes.

"April, you're going to burn yourself out, girl! Enjoy yourself. This is your day!"

I nodded. I knew he was right. All I wanted to do was to pour myself a gin to calm the nerves, but I had to settle with lemonade.

"It's turned out to be a good do," a voice near me said.

I placed the lemonade back down on the table, trying to understand why I recognised that voice. I realised when I turned myself around.

"Henry?"

Why is he here? What if Casey sees…

"Happy to see you too," he laughed. "Casey invited me. I hope you don't mind."

A sigh of relief…

"Not at all. He just never mentioned it to me." Still confused, I hugged him to draw away from the awkward greeting.

"I suppose it's congratulations, Mrs April Woods." His face screwed up, hearing it out loud for the very first time. "Sounds like a-"

"Made up name? Or perhaps a name given by a hated parent? I know." I laughed to save him from having to say it himself.

I hid my face in my glass, knocking back lemonade like a shot as quickly as I could. My eyes met with his again.

Why does he keep staring?

I put on a fake cough to put an end to the stare and turned my back to him, placing my cup back down on the table.

"Well, it's been a pleasure seeing you again, Mrs Woods. I'll let you enjoy your evening." He lumberingly left, taking a hint from my silent tone of dismissal.

I exhaled and straightened myself to disregard any thoughts running through my mind. Today is not a day to worry or overthink. Stop and just enjoy. I practiced pulling a natural smile as I glanced around to make sure no one was looking.

"Where's my red?" I heard Casey call for my attention through the singer's microphone. Waving my arm in the air I revealed myself to him in the crowd.

"There's my woman!" he embarrassingly continued talking through the microphone for all to hear.

"Would you join me in a first dance?" he asked in an eager manner.

Everyone began clapping and parting a path for me to make my way to the band's stage. Casey sat waiting in his wheelchair. As I approached him, he began lifting himself from the chair, weakly. I attempted to provide a helping hand, but he dismissed the offer, wanting to do this for himself. I let him lean some of his weight onto me. Although I was pregnant, I didn't mind. His body had become frail and weightless, but his eyes were still the same man that I fell in love with. His eyes were my primary focus. That was until I noticed Bernie and Danny move to the stage and take the microphone from the singer.

I screwed up my face for an explanation. Danny, Bernie, and Casey all laughed, as though they had conducted some evil plot prior to this.

"I asked you to just pick the first dance song to surprise me, and you never fail to surprise me, Casey." Bernie and Danny shared the microphone together, holding each other in a giggly, school kid fashion. I contagiously started laughing too, trying to control myself.

Bernie began singing and her voice echoed beautifully throughout the barn, as she started singing the lyrics to *Like I'm gonna lose you* by Meghan Trainor and John Legend. My skin tingled and the hairs on my body pricked up, in response to her well-practiced voice. Tears began flooding my eyes as I listened back to the lyrics, as though it was the first time hearing them. In this moment, it was like the song had a completely new and personal meaning. Casey cautiously followed in my footsteps, as we slow danced to the song. I could see lights flashing from my right, knowing that our audience were taking photos and videos of this moment. My lungs began drowning me with emotion, as I tried my best not to pull away and wipe the tears to try to get my breath back.

I didn't have to pull away, though, and Danny made sure of that. Like yin and yang, we managed to experience a beautiful singer before hearing a deathly pitched warble that would even make dogs howl. Danny was delighted to see laughter in the room, knowing he had fulfilled his responsibility to bring humour into the evening.

Casey removed his left arm from around my neck, bringing others in to join the dance. I leaned my head into Casey's shoulder, pulling him in close.

That was my last perfect day.

A knock at the door

I was met by familiar green eyes in close contact with my own. The wrinkles around his eyes appeared as he smiled.

"Good morning, my beautiful wife," he gracefully greeted me, before rolling back onto his side of the bed.

"How many days is this going to go on for?" I asked, while rubbing my eyes hard enough to see black dots in the distance.

"Every. Single. Day," he honestly replied, with a tone of humour.

He lay on his side, holding his head up on his hand to look longingly at me. At first it was pleasant, but he didn't break the stare, leaving me uncomfortable and hiding under the duvet for protection.

"I was thinking about taking a walk down Biddulph Grange Country Park today… You and me." Casey lay waiting for me to respond.

I slowly uncovered myself from under the covers, cocking my head to one side, staring back at him.

"But we have so much we need to do today in the baby's room."

"And we will get around to it, but I really fancy a bit of a walk. Maybe even venture from my wheelchair for a bit," he pleaded.

I could get it. His independence had been taken from him. Recently, I have had to keep a closer eye on him, as he tried to do more than he could handle. His stubborn ways still there. I reluctantly agreed. In wishful thoughts, we could have breakfast, followed by a nice short walk. At least then I would still have time this afternoon for decoration.

Casey's eyes lit up when I agreed. It made me feel grateful that even with all our uncertainties, this man was still able to smile his way through tough times.

I pulled out the wheelchair and watched as Casey's excited features faded into reality again. It was as though he still wasn't used to the idea of relying on others to assist him in simple activities, like walking. His head hung low with embarrassment, and it pained me to witness it.

I too lowered my head to his level, trying to meet with his eyes.

"Hey!" I got his attention to stand up level with me again.

"If you sit in the wheelchair, I'll make sure to let go of the handles when we go downhill. I'll even time it just to see how long it takes you to reach the bottom." I pulled the biggest smile I could, just to even get a split second of a smirk from him.

"You should get one too and we'll have a race!" He thankfully returned the humour.

Even though I saw the pain draw out his personality, there were still moments when I was able to talk to the real Casey. I was able to bring the humorous, confident man back out again.

It is right what they say – Walking helps your mental health. Taking a step away from society and into nature's arms, makes all the bad thoughts pass temporarily. For some moments, we stopped, and Casey would stand from his wheelchair to feel in tune with nature. He leaned into a large, old tree, staring directly at me. His eyes pierced through me, making me feel alive again and wanting. He boldly pulled half a smirk as I bit onto my bottom lip lightly and tightened my grip around the handles of the wheelchair.

"The same tree will never look the same as it did the day before. They're always changing," Casey said while looking up through the tall branches that spread out above him.

My heart stopped momentarily to hear those words again in my head.

"My dad used to say the exact same thing!" I responded with surprise.

Casey chuckled to himself, looking back at me with those daring eyes.

"So did mine," he warmly expressed.

I applied the brakes to the wheelchair and walked slowly over to Casey, burying my head into his chest and holding onto him, wishing forever.

"A lot has changed with this tree, since you had a photo next to it with Bernadette."

I cleared my throat and looked up at him inquisitively; my eyebrows narrowed. He laughed and proceeded to kiss my forehead. His hands wrapped around my body and his lips didn't part from my skin.

"You've changed a lot since that day too. I've seen you mature and finally come out of your shell. I've managed to see the real April and I wouldn't wish for anything else." He expressed an outburst of appreciation for everything he had in that moment and we both stood against that tree for what felt like hours before returning home again.

Once we had returned home, I dismantled the wheelchair to put it away again.

"Casey, would you like a drink?" I said whilst on my knees, tucking the chair behind the hoover and mop.

That's strange, no answer...

Struggling to stand back on my feet, I leaned my right hand against the wall to lift myself, while my left hand cradled my bump. I felt something brush my skin softly and I jumped to turn around.

"You scared me." I slapped Casey's arm.

Without words, Casey used the wall behind me as support to kneel down against my bump. His hand caressed my stomach in a circular motion, whilst feeling his warm exhalation whispering against my skin.

"Twinkle, twinkle little star," he sang.

"What are you doing?" I giggled.

"I think I should sing him a nursery song at least once, shouldn't I?" He looked back up at me with a dark undertone to his reasoning.

I crossed my arms above my bump, looking away. For too long I had been trying to keep the positive bubble afloat for both of us, and the harder I tried to float above, the harder Casey tried to follow with a sharp needle.

His sweet, soft kisses pressed against my belly in apology.

"When you're born, I'll be there. Your dad will be there to sing you all the nursery rhymes." His voice began to soften to a whisper. "I can't wait to meet you."

Groaning, he steadied himself to a stand, silently apologising to me again, as he stared back into my eyes.

"Shall we go upstairs?" he whispered into my ear, following it with a caring kiss to my forehead.

I nestled my head into his chest, nodding slowly. We helped each other up the stairs to our bed, where we peacefully fell into a sleep, holding each other close.

***

Every day we are one day closer to death. For some, Death is cruel. He will dwell around a living person, watching them enjoy their life and day by day he will absorb a little more of their soul until there is very little left to even recognise the person anymore. Watching someone slowly become more confused, forgetful or depressed is one of the harder experiences to suffer by. The person may be dead before they have even died.

But it's when you have those meaningful moments right at the end. The person you once knew looks at you intensely and recognises you. You see their true self come back for a short time before being taken away once again. It's those short moments that must be cherished. Remember them for who they were, not what they have become.

That is how I felt when I was awoken that night to the sound of ragged breathing and a distant man lying beside me in bed.

"Casey!" I shouted at him, as though it would bring him back around to me again.

Everything moved so quickly and frantically following that moment that I had no time to think. Casey was rushed into hospital and my parents soon followed to support me while we waited. I needed to hear some news, but my mum didn't help when holding me saying "everything will be ok". I felt like pushing her away and screaming that it was not ok and it's not going to be ok. My husband was dying, and the stress was not healthy for my little boy.

I tried to remain controlled, biting hold of my tongue to stay silent.

All of that anger was about to change when the doctor left the room with his face straightened with an obvious look of sympathy drawn all over his face. Hearing the news for the first time that we may have only hours left with Casey made me let go from biting my tongue. Instead, my throat became swollen, my lungs weighed down on my stomach, bringing me to my knees in weakness. I was unable to stand again as my parents wrapped themselves around me. This time, my mother didn't try to give me encouraging words. Instead, she stroked my red hair and wiped the tears from my eyes silently.

I didn't go in the room to see Casey until my cries became silent. I didn't want Casey to see that I had lost all hope for him. As I walked into the room, I saw that his heart monitor was stabilised, but his breathing was still ragged. They had managed to drain the fluid from his lungs again, but the death rattle had appeared. Death was sitting right next to Casey, looking at the final jigsaw piece to his broken soul.

I was scared to leave Casey's side in case Death saw his opportunity alone with Casey to talk to him and encourage him to leave this mortal world.

Our little bouncing baby boy was dancing on top of my bladder. I tried to hold back as much as I could before I couldn't bear it any longer.

I stroked Casey's hand, standing from my chair. Leaning over, I kissed Casey gently on the forehead.

"You promised me you'll stay around to see our little boy. Please don't leave, not yet."

I was happy to see he was still resting when I returned from the toilets. I resumed my seating position, looking at every little detail. The room itself consisted of four walls, and not one wall had any personality. No colour, no pictures, no marks, just four plain walls that didn't want to hold the memory of the person sleeping in it. Why would it? If it remains plain, it doesn't have to strip back its surface and start fresh again for the next person to visit. It remains a solemn place. The only colour this room had was the flowers and gifts that stood next to the single bed.

Casey lay in that bed with his skin as pale as the surface of the walls that surrounded him. Holding onto his hand, I prayed that Casey would stay healthy for a little while longer because I didn't want to let him go.

Is that selfish of me?

Is it selfish of me for wanting him to stay in this world for longer? I have seen this man deteriorate more and more in the last few weeks. It pains me to see him suffer day by day. If a beloved pet dog was like this, it would be wrong of the owner to keep it alive. You would want it to finally have peace.

Maybe my prayer is selfish after all…

My eyes clenched tightly in prayer, trying to hold back from the tears, until I exhausted myself. My eyes softened and I lay my head against Casey's rattling ribcage.

A cold sweat-like sensation travelled through my body, as I gently opened my eyes to see my body surrounded by water. I found myself in a lake with my blood-stained white dress sticking to the figure of my body. The stag nuzzled my chest, clearing away the blood with the pure water. I pulled out the neck of my dress, looking down at my naked wet body to see no wounds, only dirt and blood that remained stained to my dress. I exhaled with relief, holding my arms tightly to my chest to stay warm.

The trees surrounding the lake whistled and blew to the north, dragging a current of water in the same direction. The stones at the bottom of the lake were visible and I could see where the water would deepen further into the centre. I gently kicked my feet at the bottom of the water, feeling the freedom rushing through me. I finally managed to gleam a smile, taking a deep inhale. This quickly surpassed as my exhale became abruptly choked upon noticing the clear water turn to a deep red.

The stag! His wounds had not vanished like my own. I swam closer to the stag, hushing away his small cries. His legs tried to move back and forth to keep afloat, but the pain became too unbearable. I tried to wrap my arm around the stag's neck to bring him to shore, but the stag refused.

I tried to scream and cry, to beg him to follow me, but it was no use; he chose his fate. The stag's eyes didn't look in panic, but they reflected the green leaves of the surrounding trees. I watched silently, accepting his decision. The stag released his last long exhale above the depths of the water, which danced through the frost-bitten sky. His breath revealed a young girl and stag bowing to each other in a new-found greeting. The bowing stag stood upright, looking back across the lake to a father and mother, waiting patiently for their son to return home with open arms. The stag looked back at the girl once more, providing a silent appreciation and happiness for their meeting before returning across the lake to the mother and father. The breath of a once living stag faded away into the mist of clouds above that covered the living below.

My arms longingly remained opened, awaiting the stag to return to me, as I held onto my pain silently. My arms began to ache, upon realising the stag did not resurface. The clouds above became too heavy to hold on to the loss and shed its tears across the body of water, creating a memorable melody. The droplets became heavier until the melody became an abrupt noise of one long key being played.

beep

A sharp inhale brought me to consciousness again as I no longer heard difficult breathing sounding from Casey's chest. I could no longer see the green light beaming from his eyes, only the green flat line that appeared on his heart monitor.

"Nurse!" I bellowed from my sunken lungs as I ran from the room, collapsing at the door.

Everything from that moment felt as if it was moving in slow-motion, as I pleaded silently to see help arrive in the corridor. When I did hear movement closing in, I could not see a figure for the tears that flooded from my eyes.

They tried to bring Casey back to me, but he had already made his choice. I was just unable to accept it.

Written words won't bring him back

My parents believed it was best for me to stay at theirs for a while, so I wouldn't be home alone. Truth is, I don't think they trusted me not to do anything stupid. They were right.

The first stage hit me hard, denial. My mind wandered into hopeless probabilities. An afterlife, but which one? There were so many religions, it was difficult to understand what Casey's afterlife would be.

Take, for instance, Christians. The belief of heaven and hell, but who was to determine their fate? Casey was pure of heart, but he didn't believe. Would their God allow him into heaven if he didn't believe?

What about Jehovah's Witnesses? The belief that once we have died, we are dust. From dust you came, and dust you will return. That is, until Armageddon and a paradise Earth, whereby Jehovah will restore faith and humanity, bringing back those that have also perished.

Another example is the belief of reincarnation. Will I see Casey again in the form of a new life? Even if it was possible, there was no way of being able to determine if it would be my Casey.

My nights became sleepless, and my days became long and bitter. I cradled our little baby boy for the only form of silent and bearable comfort.

My mind became empty of words, as I tried longingly to write a eulogy for my husband, who had been taken from me far too soon.

The pencil lead came into contact with the paper, but the lead crumbled under the pressure of my hand angrily driving it into the desk beneath. I sharpened the pencil again, repeating the same process before tearing the paper and chucking it across the room in a pathetic attempt to get it into the bin.

I heard a quiet, terrified knock against my old bedroom door, as my mum cautiously entered with a cup of tea. She smiled, seeing my anger with a piece of paper. She gently placed the cup next to my shaking hand. She held onto my hand for comfort, as I broke into a thousand tears that soaked into the blank paper.

Holding my head to her chest, my mother swayed me slowly.

"Write it for him, not for you," she whispered into my ear, completing the sentiment with a kiss.

She left the room as quietly as she entered, and I felt her warm words take effect. I put the pencil away and pulled out a biro from my pen pot.

My eulogy to Casey Woods.

If you are joining us today, I shouldn't need to explain my story with Casey because you already know it. If you don't know our story, you didn't know Casey and probably shouldn't be here.

I will always remember one of the first sayings that Casey said to me. It was one of many, but I always remembered it. "Don't let the anchor be your burden". Casey was always full of happiness and spread that with his humour right through to the end. He never let anything hold him down to the bottom of the sea where he couldn't escape to freedom. He always pushed forward to be the best version of Casey that he could be. I am sure that if Casey was here, he would also thank all of our friends and my parents for all their motivation when times did become tough.

I struggle to open my eyes, coming to the realisation that Casey is no longer here, but every single time I close my eyes, I see him. As long as my memory does not fade, neither will he.

The words started to blur on the page as tears began to fall again. I couldn't write anymore. I placed the pencil down on its side over my heart-felt words and pulled my chair away from the desk, howling into my hands once again.

"Goldie! You've got a delivery!" I heard my father shout up the stairs to me, with nothing but gentleness in his tone.

I cleared my throat, leaving my room for the first time that day.

"Seems to be some flowers, love. It's got no message on. Has somebody sent these to you?"

My father held up nicely presented white egret orchids in a grey ceramic pot.

"I ordered them for myself," I croaked through my clogged throat.

Carrying the flowers back up to my room, I felt the silk-like petals of the white orchid between my fingertips. I placed them on my bedroom windowsill as a temporary placement, before taking them back to my own home.

***

On the day of the funeral, I wore my mother's old black maternity dress that hung down to my knees, bringing out my pale skin and baggy eyes from sleepless nights. I hated being alone with my own thoughts, but I also hated having company. I cried when on my own, but I also cried when bringing Casey into conversation with others.

My parents said how talking will help bring closure and after some time it did, but not at that time. I tried to apply just a little mascara to bring colour back to my eyes, but at every attempt, a new tear would shed, creating a murky mess running across my red cheeks. I wiped away the makeup, accepting that I will need to stay natural.

Close friends met at my parent's home before we departed to a nearby church where my grandparents were also buried. They all tried to talk to me, and I tried to interact, but my voice would break. I instinctively leaned in for a comforting hug instead.

If I can't talk now, I will never be able to do the eulogy!

The vicar stood at the altar of the church with his head held high, talking of Casey as if he had known him his entire life. He didn't know Casey and looking behind at the other people sat at the available pews, a lot of the people in attendance didn't truly know him either. They probably didn't even know who I was.

Then my time came...

I needed to wee now more than ever, even though I had gone to the toilet just before we had arrived. I became light-headed as I approached the front. My hands messed with the belt that was tied in a bow above my baby bump. I began rolling the belt up, as though it was causing me discomfort. In reality, I didn't want people to stare at the girl with the little black dress, red hair and pregnant belly walking down before the statue of Jesus hanging on a cross.

I turned to face my audience, but kept my head held down. Reaching for the folded piece of paper in my pocket, I mentally tried to prepare myself. The paper looked worn, like I had put it through a wash cycle before arriving. I knew what I wanted to say, but it somehow became difficult to speak without reading from a piece of paper, like a script that should have been memorised weeks beforehand.

"If you are joining us today, I shouldn't need to explain my story with Casey because you already know it. If you don't know our story, you didn't know Casey and probably shouldn't be here."

I looked to my mother who sat in the front row, looking anxious. I blurred the others from my vision and kept looking at my mother, my rock. A tear fell from my eyes and upon realising, she smiled with a tear dripping against her cheek, nodding me to go on, for Casey.

It is moments like this when you hold your parents close to your heart. All the fights, shouting and disagreements become extracted from your mind, as you quickly appreciate how many other times they had been there as your supporting bridge to cross to a greener path.

I cleared my throat, smiling at my mother.

"But all of you are here and there is a reason for that. Perhaps you played with him in a school football match, or he told you something once that has always stuck to you. No matter the reason, I know Casey would be proud of you all, for not mourning his death, but celebrating the life in which he had."

My parents' faces gleamed, and their hands held together tightly, forming a stronger bond than ever before. I took a deep inhale, before releasing a quivering exhale and continued with the remainder of my speech.

I felt that I had achieved a newfound strength as I remained calm, without collapsing in that very room. That was until they lowered his coffin into the ground. Casey is in that box alone and is to be buried six feet under, away from everyone. Somewhere where I will never be able to see the smile on his face again. The realisation that he is no longer on this Earth with me, but now resides in the earth among its encroaching roots.

"April, we're going for some food. You should join us," I heard Bernadette reach out with Danny in her arms.

"I will. I just need some time alone with Casey." I didn't even look back as I knelt down beside the headstone.

"When you're ready..." Bernadette acknowledged before leaving with Danny to the pub.

It was finally silent, except for the wind that brushed past my hair, carrying my cries into the dark sky. I stroked the stone carvings of his name, our name. Anger and pain shot through my aching body.

"You promised!" I hit my fist against the soil before expressing my emotions into the mound of dirt that now covered him as a forever blanket.

I reached into my pocket once more, bringing out a white egret orchid flower that I had cut from its stem earlier that morning. With two fingers, I made an indent in the soil, placing the flower above him. I kissed the white petals, tainting it with my darkened lipstick. The rest of the words, I told him in my head, in hopes that he would somehow hear me and how much I still needed him in this world with me.

You will always be a red wine stain that I will never be able to remove from my white wedding dress, Casey Woods...

Night brings a new life

They tell you funerals are supposed to bring closure, but they don't. Funerals are just a way of forcing you to accept that they have truly gone from this world, never to be seen again. That thought churned my stomach every single time I opened my eyes to see that Casey was no longer in this world.

On the occasions when I had managed to close my eyes, my dreams were barren. I'd see my own body still staying afloat in an empty lake. Not even the wind whistled soothing words to me. Was this version of myself waiting for something? Or had she lost the motivation to move forward? She wouldn't speak or even look anywhere except at the bottom of the lake.

After speaking to my midwife about the recent news, she encouraged me to seek help from a mental health service at her recommendation. I did consider taking the offer, but the thought of speaking out about this so early on brought me to tears just thinking about it. I struggled enough to speak to my parents and our friends as it was.

My phone had to be placed on silent due to the number of calls and texts I would receive from my closest friends and even from numbers that I didn't recognise. At first, I tried my hardest to reply, but other days I struggled to keep up. On the quiet days, I would usually see Bernadette call by to check in on me. We tried to steer away from the elephant in the room and focus on better things, but everything always had a link to Casey in one way or another.

"Hi, baby girl!" Bernadette hollered, as she swung my parents' front door open with her arms spread out for a hug.

I managed to force a smile, waddling over, imposing a reciprocated greeting.

"I can barely hug you with the little guy third wheeling between us."

That comment did make me laugh. It wasn't much of a laugh, but it was a step forward in the right direction. My parents welcomed Bernadette into their home, asking if she would stop for tea. Their offer was more like a beg to stay and help me, but I acted oblivious for the sakes of my parents. Bernie's face straightened as she looked down at her phone, as though she already had plans. She looked back up at me and my parents, who waited desperately for an answer. Bernadette's frown relaxed, and she returned to me with a softening smile.

"I'll stay," she replied, followed by a moment of appreciation from my parents.

Having Bernadette at the dinner table encouraged me to speak out a bit more. She brought back memories of our teenage lives, cutting some parts of the memories from the equation, knowing my parents wouldn't approve. Bernadette would always fill in the blanks by raising her eyebrows at me and smiling, before moving onto the next chapter of the memory.

Squeezing tight on the sofa, we all sat together watching a family film until late. I can't remember the film we watched that night, but I remember closing my eyes and falling asleep on Bernie's shoulder before the film had even finished.

I saw myself in the lake again. This time, the sun had finally arisen after nights of continued darkness. The lake became clear once more. Fish swam with the current, taking them upstream. My dress was no longer stained, but a clean white that spread its tail on the surface of the water. The wind whistled sweet melodies through the branches of the trees, bringing forward hope again. I closed my eyes from the glare of the sun, allowing myself to be drawn under the water. I held my breath at the bottom of the lake, crossing my legs as if I was meditating.

I opened my eyes once more, looking across into the depths at the fish swimming close by. Holding out my hand to feel the scales, I pulled back, noticing the hands of a young girl... The body of a young girl. I expelled breath, causing a fluctuation of bubbles to rise to the surface of the water. My body floated to the surface with the bubbles, appearing out of the water.

"Are you okay, April?" I heard Bernadette ask with a disturbed early morning croak in her voice.

The room was dark, and I was still on the sofa with just Bernadette and a blanket keeping us warm. I felt a wet sensation between my legs.

"Great! Now I've lost control of my bladder too," I laughed at my loss of control.

"Are you sure your waters haven't broken?" Bernie asked with a concerned tone.

I chuckled at first, before realising her cause for concern.

"I'm only thirty-five weeks Bernie, I can't be…" I responded, trying to reassure her of the situation.

Bernadette continued to remain concerned, removing the blanket from me and looking at the large wet patch that soaked into the sofa. Embarrassed, I crossed my legs tightly, trying to draw her attention away from it.

"April, it doesn't smell like urine… Maybe try standing and sitting down again."

I didn't move, but instead responded with a face of uncertainty.

"If you stand and sit down again and you still have fluid dripping, it's not going to be urine. Please try."

Her concern reflected on me, as I no longer felt embarrassed by a loss of control, but in fear that my baby was too early to be born. I stood up slowly and a little fluid dripped again, but that could have just been a little more urine in my urethra… I hope. I sat down slowly and repeated the process.

It's still going…

Silently, I looked at Bernadette with fear echoing through my body.

"Mike! Lorraine! We need you!" Bernadette screamed at the top of her lungs, as she held on to my trembling hands.

It was silent only for a moment, before I heard footsteps frantically moving on the ceiling above us.

My mother was the first to run into the room, switching the lights on and overwhelming me with questions in her moment of alarm.

"I think my waters have broken…" I answered with uncertainty and panic in my voice.

My mother and father looked to Bernadette for confirmation. Bernie slowly nodded her head in agreement.

"Mike! You need to get our daughter to the hospital, now!" my mother ordered.

"Shouldn't I call my mid-wife?" I interrupted without giving my dad a chance to answer.

"I'll sort that sweetie. You need to get to the hospital. It'll be okay. We're here with you." My mother kissed me on the forehead before running back to her bedroom to find her phone.

Whilst my parents and Bernadette frantically ran around to get everything that was needed, I remained on the sofa like I was playing a game of statues. Although my body remained still, my mind frantically ran from door to door, looking behind each one to see the other side of this story.

When arriving at the hospital, it was confirmed that I was in labour. My thoughts had built so drastically in such a short space of time that I outwardly expressed my pain. My mother, who agreed to be my birthing partner, never left my side for one moment. I let out a scream as the contractions increased the pain and the mental strain drew out of me, as though Death was taunting me for staying alive.

"Stay with me, sweetie. You're doing great. I'm here with you every step of the way." My mother's words of encouragement echoed through my body, showing me why I needed to go on.

I was exhausted, and I wanted to finally rest, but I knew I couldn't. It was like being hung from high above a fire, with only a rope to hold on to. There is still another 50 feet of rope to climb, but you're too exhausted to go on. If you stay there, your arms will begin to ache from holding the weight and you will fall to your death. You cannot go back down the rope without also facing death. The only way is to continue to climb. Through a sudden spurt of adrenaline, your body continues to climb, knowing that at the end you will have beaten death at his own game.

After hours of testing, monitoring, and pushing, my little boy finally wanted to see me.

"One last push!" My mid-wife urged me on.

That final release, knowing you have brought life into a new world, is one of the most empowering moments to experience. Hearing your baby cry for the first time brings all the other instincts to reality as you eagerly want to hold them close.

Weighing only 4lbs, his tiny body curled around my chest. His little hands stretched as I gently held them with my own. I let out a loud cry of gratefulness into the room. His eyes opened, revealing the colour of leaves from a summer alder tree. In his right eye was a speckled white dot within the green shade of his iris.

My little white orchid…

"Just like your father," I cried to my son, holding him tightly to my body.

"Have you thought of any names?" my midwife asked.

I smiled intently at his tiny body.

"Elijah."

***

More tests needed to be run on both me and Elijah to ensure we were both healthy, considering the prematurity of his birth. Although he was small and weak, he managed to fight through as strong as his father did.

I would be lying to myself if I was to say that things became easier after the birth of Elijah. Even though Elijah had distracted me from my own painful thoughts, I still saw his father every time I looked into his eyes. My own mental state had become confusing as I tried to distinguish between sadness and happiness. I found myself crying in episodes without knowing the reason why. All I knew was that I loved this boy with all my heart. He was my reason to stay strong and push forward in this cruel world.

With the support of friends and family, I managed to find the help I needed, rather than struggling as a single mother. This continued for a few months before I announced that I would be moving back to my old home. Elijah kept my parents up at night and I could see that the sleepless nights and constant help were eventually wearing them down. I needed to make that step at some point, and this was the perfect opportunity to put one foot in front of the other.

Note to reader

I originally wrote this as a way of healing myself. By the power of expression in writing itself, I am healed. I want to share this with others. This story is not one to be hidden away, and please do not think for one second that this story has ended. My story still lives on, and Elijah has provided me with purpose.

After moving back into my old home, memories rained down on me like a thunderstorm. My parents insisted on me staying a little longer, but I needed this progress. The longer I stayed away, the harder it would become to return to my old life. My mother reluctantly agreed to my decision, assisting in the move.

When it was only me and Elijah, I struggled to sleep in the double bed with one side that remained empty. Post-natal depression had set in quickly and aggressively, as I angrily collapsed in a helpless environment. I didn't want to text Bernadette or my parents to disturb or concern them, but I gripped onto hopes that they may do a surprise visit on me, so I could momentarily find myself at ease. When this didn't happen, I grew angry with my family and friends for not visiting. My body and mind were going through constant changes with a newborn. I wasn't ready to be alone and I knew that deep down, but I wanted to prove myself.

What a fool I was…

When I first started writing this novel, I was contemplating my own life when the razor looked at me with a sense of temptation. I held the razor in my bedroom, looking down at my trembling arms.

"I want to be with you, Casey!" I screamed out in pain. My fingers gripped around the razor, piercing my fingers. I didn't feel pain, but I felt a drip like sensation from my thumb down to my wrist.

Elijah began crying and the anger left my body. I noticed the blood and dropped the razor from my hand, gasping for air, wishing that I could be let free of Death's games. I grabbed some tissues from the box on my desk and wrapped it vigorously around my thumb before running to Elijah.

His green eyes beamed a brighter colour as the glaze of tears ran down his rosy cheeks. I held him up to my chest, slowly swinging my body from side to side.

"Shhh… It's okay. Mummy's here." I ran my fingers through his fine, short hair.

What was I thinking?

It was a month following that I finally broke free from depression. After considering taking my own life, I asked Bernadette to come and assist me with Elijah. I couldn't let my parents see me in this state after they had insisted I stay home with them.

I needed to bring some organisation to my life. Things to do each day to keep myself focused. Bernadette loved doing spreadsheets and graphs, so she was more than happy to put a planner together for me.

I finally agreed to seek help from a mental health service near me. I had the opportunity to express myself and cry without judgement or self-doubt. I was provided with advice (and homework) that assisted little by little to help me grow.

Bernadette routinely visited every day, even if it could only be for ten minutes, to make sure I had everything I needed. I organised days in which my parents could help me with shopping or looking after Elijah, so I could socialise with friends or take part in charity events.

I finally managed to accept and enjoy life again. There were times when I would reminisce on what life would have been like and looking back at memories, but by writing these words, I have managed to bring closure. Everything I have ever wanted to say is now written in permanent ink. These ink stains are the stains that Casey has left with this world.

I'm now no longer scared of being alone, as I sat in the living room one late evening, with a hot chocolate on the coaster beside me. I gazed over at the three wooden carvings that I ornamented in the house from Casey's proposal. Trying to hold back from tears again, I fidgeted with the rings that were fitted on my wedding finger. I reminisced on the day when I first saw those otters holding onto a wooden chest, still oblivious as to what was happening. Picking up the wooden otters, I removed the engagement ring from my finger and placed it into the box that the otters held onto dearly. I carried the box upstairs with me and slowly opened Elijah's door, to stop it from creaking. I held the carved otters close to my chest whilst the tidal waves ran from my eyes, staining the wood with my lost love. I need luck more than anything right now, to keep me moving in the right direction. My charm of luck lay resting in the cradle before me.

    I leaned over the cradle, kissing my son gently.

    "Sleep tight, Elijah."

    I came to stand, drawing my attention to the window that provided the only light into the darkened room. The night sky remained clear, showing an abundance of stars gleaming in the midst. I grasped hold of the windowsill, seeking answers in the sky above.

    "Sleep tight, Casey."

About the author:

D. B. Sherratt, otherwise known as Danielle Sherratt, is a first-time writer of this romance novel – The woods of white.

Growing up in Biddulph Moor, Danielle was inspired by her rural surroundings. This became a focal point in her romance novel.

Danielle has enjoyed writing books from the age of ten. She would often write and illustrate her own books, which she would later read to her younger sister, Annie.

She hopes that this book will reach the hearts of her readers. This novel is not to break the heart of the reader, but to provide hope even in the toughest of times. By writing in first person, the female lead expresses how to manage struggles with mental health.

D. B. Sherratt shares her accomplishments and updates on social media. You can follow her on Instagram / Facebook: D. B. Sherratt.

As a first-time author, D. B. Sherratt wants to share thanks to those who have read and enjoyed this novel.

CONTENT WARNINGS:

This story includes references to self-harm, mental illness, death, expletive and sexual content.

Printed in Great Britain
by Amazon